# The Ghost of Delbert Mucks

*D.W. Smith*

**Sandy Smith Publishing**

ISBN – 9798367278149

Cover design by: Art Painter

Library of Congress Control Number: 2018675309

Printed in the United States of America

*Index*

# *Delbert Mucks*


## Acknowledgements

The ghost of Delbert Mucks is a tall tale from the imagination of Doyle Smith.  Somethings just don't need explanations – this novel is one of them.

To Nora Ray, one of my daughters, my heart fell thanks for her unique ability to translate my Okie English, hydro graphics, and creative spelling into something readable.

And to the readers of my other works, with all my heart, thank you!

Most of all, to my Lord and Savior, for long life, good health and for the pleasure of writing this tall tale.

## *Ch. 1 Ghosts*

Now Shadey is a little berg, a way off the beaten path, in more ways than one, in Southeastern Oklahoma. Not too far from the South Canadian River.

Sometime after the civil war, the railroad up north, got authorization to lay a spur line across the south Canadian River near an old Indian settlement that eventually became known as The Little Town of Shadey. Outside of a train going through town, every once in a while, not much happened out of the ordinary in, or around Shadey.

Around Shadey, there had always been lots of Indians and their superstition. Their kin had been there since the stone age- or at least since the flood you know-what white men called Noah's Flood!

There were some folks in Shadey that were not Indian, no one seemed to know, or care, where they came from. If your ancestors were in Indian Territory of Oklahoma, before the civil war, they were either Indian or an outlaw! Most of Shadeys residents claimed being a descendent of one or the other with pride.

In Shadey there was a number of part Indians. Old Harley Fritzs, one of the local intuitions, was one of them. Now exactly which part of Harley was Indian was kinda hard to identify. Harley said he had a roll number – that made him and Indian of some tribe- despite having a light completion, blond hair, steely blue eyes and no Indian kin folks anyone in Shadey knew of.

Now the story goes, Harley Fritz's, one of the well-known Shadey residents came in Mona's Café one morning, obviously in a state of high agitation, swearing he's been attacked by a ghost!

Old Harley was having trouble telling Mona and the locals setting in Mona's Café, exactly what had happened to him between the gasps and sputters. Anyway, according to Harley something, supposedly a ghost, started talking to him from the sky, or ground, or from somewhere – and then something – maybe a ghost had hit him on back of his head to prove it!

Being as Harley had always lived in Shadey, he had never been known to tell tall tales. Mona was fairly certain, Harley had seen a ghost, and may have got whooped by one. She began to spread the word, as did some of the locals setting in Mona's café.

Now in small, close-knit communities like Shadey, Harley's ghost story spread around the community like wildfire! If Harley said it, there had to be something unusual happening, out around the cemetery. Most everybody, especially the Indians, knew if there was such a thing as a ghost. A ghost lived around dead bodies! The things about ghost are they always haunt the night, but Harley's ghost, had appeared and whopped Harley in the daytime. No one around Shadey had ever heard of such a thing.

The cemetery out near Harley's place had been a burying place – since – anyway- a way back yonder, ever since crows, ghost, and Indians had lived around Shadey. Indians were full of ghost stories, but no ghost had ever appeared in the daytime or known to whoop people before. Harley's ghost, everyone agreed, was note worthy!

Soon, Jim Bohannen, Shadeys Mayor, and Otto Shorts, one of the councilmen, came in Mona's café and sat down, and ordered breakfast. Now that Harvey had settled down somewhat, he sat down with the new arrivals and began to retell his ghost story. With intent attention, Otto and Jim, two of the towns trusted officials, hung upon every word of Harley's ghost tale. After breakfast, all three men decided to go out to Harley's place, next to cemetery, and see if some evidence of a ghost attack could be found. The three older men made their way out to Harley's place, next to the cemetery, in Otto's old truck.

On the north and east of the cemetery was a number of tall trees and dense vegetation, south was a little clearing where Harley's shack was, and west was the county road that wonders through the forest covered hills to the South Canadian River.

"I was right over yonder," said Harley, pointing at his chicken house near the stand of timber, east of the cemetery.

"I was minding my own business, just feeding my chickens, when something hollered 'Hello' – plain as day. I liked to have jumped out of my hide – I know it wasn't my chickens or Buellas – and there was an echo, - another hello! Now I was just looking around, trying to see where the hello can from, when all of a sudden this ghost whoops me on back of my head!"

The three older men just stood there, where Harley got whooped, somewhat perplexed, when off in the distance; faintly, they hear a "Hello."

"Did you hear that?" Said a now animated Otto. "I heard that ghost' said Jim "and I heard an echo too! Another hello – I think I heard something else too – did something say Delbert?"

"I heard something else to," said Otto cupping his ear. "Couldn't quite make it out."

"See I told you!" said Harley, "there ghosts out here – in the day no less! Right over yonder is where they buried Muck's bones!"

That afternoon, the cemetery had a half dozen ghost hunters trying to hear with their own ears – the sounds from the sky- or maybe those 'Hellos' came from the ground!

Outside of Harley and his two friends no one else, that day, had admitted to hearing the ghost of Delbert Mucks, but it soon became an excepted fact there were ghosts – in the daytime – out around Shadeys Cemetery – It had to be Mucks ghost!

## *Ch. 2 The Investigation*

If you traveled on down the county road a mile or so, passed the old Shadeys cemetery, over on the west side, was a gate seldom used, weed strong lane beneath a canopy of overhanging trees. At the end of that lane was a little clearing with an old, abandoned shack, and a couple of falling down out building, and a little garden spot. Delbert Mucks, the old recluse used to live there.

Delbert Mucks had been dead, some say, at least six months before the constable, Buford Nitch, found an unsigned anonymous note stuck in the constable's office door, saying that there was a dead body in the floor out at that old shack north of town where that old hermit lived.

Now Buford made his way out to old Delbert's shack, obviously, the old road hadn't been used in quite some time. After parking his car, Buford took careful note of his surroundings, making sure his service piece was all unbridled. After casually stepping upon the decaying porch, Buford gave a police knock on the side of the old shack, hollering loudly, "Hello – Hello anybody home?" After a pause, from somewhere, came a faint 'hello' and a fluttering sound.

Somewhat apprehensive, Buford carefully, pushed open the door, and peeked in, making sure his service piece was unstrapped. Sure enough, there in the floor was a decaying, stinking, human body – at least, what was left of it!

After retrieving his camera from his car, Buford Nitch, began his investigation. After photographing the dead body, and its surroundings, Buford began to rummage through the old shack, taking more pictures.

Up against the wall was an old dresser with some old rags that used to be clothes. Hanging on a nail nearby, was an old change of clothes. There was an old cot with a woman's picture hanging nearby. The old wood burning stove, with a cooking pot, and a lid, held what might have been food. There were some dishes, a small table with an open notebook, with some writing about something at the lab. There wasn't much of anything else, except for a stack of papers, over in a corner.

Out back was, what might have been a chicken house, and an outhouse. Standing on the small back porch, near an old rocking chair, he could see the water well and a small garden plot, now overgrown with weeds – and in a large tree over shadowing Mucks shack was a good number of now arriving crows.

What happened next, Buford wasn't too sure of, nor did it seem to be something he wanted to talk about. Looking up at the crows, now lining up in the tree, somewhat surprised, Buford muttered – "Well hello there."

There seemed to be a couple of "Hellos" from somewhere – and then – a good half dozen crows lit right in front of the porch where Buford stood. What happened next was even harder to believe – those crows, before him, flopped upside down – spread their wings and began to plead; "Please, Please, Please".

Not sure of what had just happened, somewhat startled Buford went back into the house, in a hurry, slammed the back door, sped past the decaying body, slammed the front door, got into his car and went back to Shadey –Somewhat Shaken!

Back in town, now, kinda settled down, Buford continued his investigation. Several of Shadeys citizens were standing around at Gus Gas Station. No one could remember having a conversation with the old recluse. When Mucks came to town, he pushed his wheelbarrow, oh so slow into town, got some goods sold at the mercantile, went to the post office and left town.

If you wanted to know anything, about anything, Mona's Café was a good place to start. Bruce Adams, owner of the Shadey Mercantile and Grocery, was having dinner with Jim Bohannen, the mayor and Otto Shorts, one of the city councilmen and Harley Fritzs was settled near by ease dropping. Buford came in Mona's Café set down with the mayor and councilmen, ordered his dinner and began to continue his questioning of the local citizens.

Bruce Adams, owner of the Shadey Mercantile and Grocery, said he'd never heard one word out of Mucks mouth except to say what he wanted. Bruce said, "Old Mucks never volunteered any conversation, nor did I see any necessity to make small talk with a stinking, cash paying, unfriendly customer".

Then Bruce added, "The only thing unusual about Mucks purchases was the amount of notebook paper, pencils, and feed corn he bought – always in cash, usually in ten-dollar bills.

As far as anyone knew, Mucks didn't have no livestock – not even chickens! How anyone could live out in the country-without chickens – was unheard of. "Of course, with Mucks dead maybe six months, his chickens could have run off or got critter ate" said the one-time farmer, Otto Shorts.

It was common practice, to stay away from folk in small, out of the way, communities like Shadey, with lots of Indian influence. Every household had a loaded varmint gun, and folks who knew how to use one. That left everyone to their own business. Local folks were reluctant to infringe upon another's living space, unless they knew you. That was another one of those Indian things. Maybe that explained how old Delbert Mucks, if that was his name, could be dead maybe some six months before anyone knew about it.

That old hermit had lived out there in that old shack, as long as anyone around Shadey could remember – some of the old timers said maybe 30 years.

After dinner down at Mona's Café, after making numerous inquiries, Buford made it over to the post office.

"Miss Johns," ask Buford "Did old Muck even get any mail?"

"Oh, now and then, he got a letter" said Miss Johns, "the thing was Mucks letters never had a return address, so's I could send them back, but eventually old Muck would come in and request any mail for Delbert Mucks. Sometimes they'd be a letter or two, sometimes not. There was usually post marked Reachen Oklahoma, sometimes from some place back east."

"Miss Johns" asked the constable, "Did old Delbert ever mail a letter when he came into the post office?"

"Well" said Miss Johns, "There was that one time – a year or so ago – best I can recollect – when old Mucks mailed this big envelope. I had to charge him extra postage – it seems, best I can recollect - it was addressed to some school back east. I kinda thought that 'that's odd. Mucks didn't look like nobody that knowed nothing about no school."

"Was that the only time?" ask Buford.

"Well, there were some other times, way back yonder," said Miss Johns, kinda looking a far off. "Best I can recollect, all he ever mailed was big letters – you know big envelopes."

"Uh Huh," said Buford, "You have any idea what was in those packets?"

"Just papers – I guess" said Miss Johns, seemingly in deep thought, then she added, "Best I recollect – oh – it seemed to me – now that I recollect –some of them big letters were addressed to somebody in some bird department, in some school back east. I kinda thought that was odd – but then again everything about Mucks was odd – best I recollect."

"Did Mr. Mucks get any mail lately?" asked the constable.

"I'll see" said Miss Johns, as she searched a stack of mail. "Here, that's one letter, addressed to Delbert Munks."

"I'll take it," said Buford.

"Ok" said Miss Johns. "Mucks ain't gonna come after his mail no more and I can't return it."

Buford came back to his office. Jim Bohannen, Shadeys Mayor, and Otto Shorts, the councilman was waiting for the constable return.

"I got Mucks mail," said Buford. "There was a letter over at the post office addressed to Delbert Mucks – maybe it will shed some light on who he was."

There in front of witnesses Buford opened the letter – the letter contained three crisp, new, ten dollar bills – and a little unsigned note, "See you soon dear."

It was decided by the constable and the city fathers, Otto Shorts, Jim Bohannen and Bruce Adams, that the thirty dollars would probably cover the cost of Moses, the towns handyman, to gather the remains of old dead Delbert Mucks, and bury them out by the east fence, in the Shadey Cemetery. That was that – nothing else was needed to be done until the body was gone.

Later, down at Mona's Café someone overheard Buford say, "Maybe a ghost lived out there. I don't see how any human could live in squander like that. There wasn't anything worth stealing except a few canned goods over on a shelf, and a stack of paper in the corner. Probably saved for kindling, I guess that stuff will rot where it's at."

<<>><<>><<>>

Harley Fritzs and his Indian wife Buella, lived in the house in the little clearing south of the cemetery. They had lived there for years. They set-up housekeeping over by the cemetery just before the Vietnam War started, and raised some renegade kids there, on that old homestead that used to be Indian land. The kids, now grown, had moved on to greener pastures, and left Harley and Buella to fend for themselves.

The Fritzs' had lived there for years and never had any trouble with ghosts until old Moses, the towns handyman, had gathered up the bones of Delbert Mucks and buried them right next to the cemetery fence.

Moses, the town's handyman, was also the towns drunk. For the thirty dollars Buford gave him, Moses took a tow sack and a shovel with him out to the Mucks place. Moses shoveled old Mucks body into the tow sack, appropriated Muck's wheelbarrow, and wheeled the remains out to the cemetery – by then - Moses had about emptied his jug of spirits.

Harley and Buella watched the burying of Delbert Mucks from their kitchen window. By now Moses was a really drunk Indian.

Moses had dug a nice deep hole out by the cemetery's east fence before he went to get Mucks remains. Moses staggered through the cemetery gate, then pushed the wheelbarrow across several graves, and got to the freshly dug hole. Moses paused at the grave site, took a swig of his happy juice, and tossed the bottle in the hole. After a few moments of seemingly confusion, Moses up ended the wheelbarrow dumping the body into the grave. After farther consideration, Moses turned the wheelbarrow upside down on top of the body, and began to shovel the dirt back into the hole – all the while singing or chanting some Indian war hoop. Moses finished covering the hole, danced around the grave a few times, and then staggered back to Shadey to sober up in Buford's jail. All the activity was duly reported by Harley, down at Mona's Café.

It was common knowledge around Shadey, that area, set aside by the east fence was for bodies buried at the town's expense. Over the years, a couple of hobos had been found out by the railroad bridge. Molly Grubs, on one of her trips to Shadey, had reported a body there on the river's edge. It had been there quite a while. Old Moses, the towns drunk, served as the town's undertaker on these occasions.

As far as anyone knew, Mucks didn't have any kin, so it was appropriate to have Moses bury the old recluse Mucks, out by the east fence. There didn't seem to be any need for a Christian burial for such a burden on society, or on the town's limited budget.

<<>><<>><<>>

A day or two after the Mucks burial, Buford and Jim decided to go out to the old house. Buford took a few more pictures while Jim went outback, to investigate the chicken house and out house.

There were a number of crows in the tree near old Mucks shack. While looking around the chicken house, in a cage, was a couple of dead birds, maybe crows, beyond that, nothing deemed out of the ordinary. Looking toward the strand of trees, west of the chicken house, a number of crows were evident. Now and then there was a faint, barely audible sound from the tree tops that Jim dismissed as the wind blowing.

Both men now satisfied, nothing was amiss, went back to Shadey. Delbert Mucks, now out of sight, would soon be forgotten.

"Did you hear them crows talking?" asked Buford, on their way back to town.

"I couldn't make it out, said Jim. "My hearing ain't as good as it once was. I just thought it was the wind blowing."

"Sounded like talk to me," said Buford – "Probably Mucks ghost."

## *Ch. 3 Business as Usual*

Now Buella Fritzs was an Indian of some sort, and she looked like an Indian squaw. She always wore traditional Indian, bright colored clothing with lots of Indian jewelry. Those one hundred sixty acres of the Fritzs homestead was part of Buella traditional tribe land – and the cemetery held many of her ancestors. Buella kept watch, that none of her buried ancestor's graves were disturbed by archeologist, vandals, evil spirits or ghost.

Buella was rarely seen off the Fritzs place, but Harley was seen around town on a regular basis – Especially at Mona's Café. Harley was one of those gadabouts that knew everybody, and everybody knew Harley. Harley always kept up on the latest gossip.

Like a lot of Indians in the community, the Fritzs had resided in that location several generations. When Buella, showing up with her blue-eyed fair complexion man, it raised a few eyebrows. In the Indian reservation out east of Shadey, back in time, Harley identified himself as an Indian with a roll number, - that made him an Indian.

When lots of oil, was discovered on Indian land up in Seminole County, and later, another oil bonanza was developed near Fittstown, in Pontotoc County, Indians found prosperity. Now Indians got an allotment of government commodities, an Indian clinic was built up in Pontotoc County, Indian welfare services became available, and some Indians could get a little monthly oil check too.

Indians didn't have to work to stay alive – like other folks – and Harley Fritzs had never had a job anyone knew about. That wasn't unusual around Shadey, if you were Indian. If you wasn't Indian you had a job, or you was a poor red dirt farmer or a moonshiner.

The old recluse, Delbert Mucks didn't fit Shadeys mold of the local citizen. He'd never worked, wasn't Indian, didn't moonshine, despite buying lots of corn feed, always in cash, and he was never seen around any of Shadeys civic functions. Mucks had set up his residency in that old shack years ago – he never bothered anybody – Mucks just existed. – Usually out of sight – and out of mind.

It had been suggested, in the Indian community, that old Mucks wasn't even human. As elusive as he was, they said "He might be an evil spirit," to some, he was a reminder of white man's indifference to Indian affairs, - after stealing their tribal lands!

Mucks looked and smelled more dead than alive, especially in summer, when he'd wheeled into town, pushing his wheelbarrow. Every month or two, sometimes three, he'd buy his goods down at Bruce Adams Store, go to the post office, and push his wheelbarrow back down main street, in full view, of everybody in town, and back out to that old shack. That routine had been observed in Shadey by Shadeys citizens for years – some old timers said since the Korean War ended in 1953.

There are some people that regular folks stay away from. Delbert Mucks was one of those people. It was common practice to stay away from what you don't know nothing about. Outside of the fact, someone had found old Mucks dead out there in that shack and reported it, not much attention was generated by the Mucks affair- until Mucks ghost became a reality around Shadey.

Rumors had it, that note that got stuck in the constable, Buford Nitch's door, came from the DEAD! That note was stuck in the door by Mucks ghost or by one of those old black crow demons that always congregated around evil dens of inequality, and dead bodies.

There were crows – lots of crows in the country around Shadey. Everyone knew there was a staggering crow congregation out north of Shadey, right near the south Canadian River, around Mucks old falling down shack.

How, or why, crows in large numbers congregate near Mucks place was a local community curiosity, no one had an answer to – nevertheless – an established fact! Mucks had to be a devil, if not the devil! Those crows were now the devils' disciples – it just made sense – folks fear most, what they understand the least. That unusual crow behavior wasn't very assuring.

Old Delbert Mucks was dead and had been buried maybe a year or so. Occasionally there would be a report surface, around Shadey of the ghost of Delbert Mucks making his appearance. When someone heard talking, from the sky, or there were some other unexplained anomalies, it was blamed on the ghost of Delbert Mucks – however - crows were usually around.

Now Buford Nitch was actually aware, but still in denial about hearing crows talk and seeing some odd behavior. Buford had heard a crow talk – maybe more than one – out at Delbert's shack when he was investigating the Mucks body, that first time – Again, maybe the second time, Buford wasn't one to talk much about the constable business – What would people think, the next election, if he said he'd heard crows talking, and reported what he'd seen?

Harley Fritzs had reported several times, down at Mona's Café, about hearing Ghost talk, ever since Moses had buried Mucks out by the east fence. Harley swore he'd heard "Hello" mentioned on several occasions while he was out feeding his chickens. He said he'd heard "Dam" - "Pretty Boy" – "Please" – and "Delbert" too. One morning Harley came in Mona's Café with another knot on his head!

"A crow done it" huffed Harley.

Mucks 'grave was right across the fence from where Harley got whopped again.

Several fishermen had come into Mona's Café saying they'd heard Muck's ghost talking, out on the river. And there had been other attacks, too!

Mockingbirds, when nesting can get rather aggressive, everybody knew that, but crows attacking humans was unheard of until Old Mucks showed up dead. Them crow demons had attacked Harley Fritzs twice! Buella Fritzs, Bubba Trots, Jessie Sims, and a couple of Indians that everybody around Shadey knew, had been crow pecked too!

On that day, right after Buella Fritzs got pecked; she came in Bruce Adam's store madder than a hornet, looking for Harley.

According to Buella, Muck's evil spirit was unsettling to her ancestors that were buried out in the cemetery.

Buella lit into Bruce Adams, a city councilman, she demanded, "I want old Mucks dug up and throwed in the river! He ain't got no business being in the same cemetery with my kin!"

Nothing else, according to Buella would pacify her dead ancestors. Buella said, "If evil spirits could make hogs jump in a lake and drown, like the Preacher said last Sunday, Mucks needed drowning too, so's those evil spirits would drown!"

"I don't think drowning Mucks would do no good now" said Bruce smiling, as he confided to Buford down at Mona's Café

It just had to be Muck's ghost that had set the crows off. Ghost or no ghost – crows attacking folks, - minding their own business – was unheard of and it had to stop! There had even been some mentioning of a crow season!

No one, down at Mona's Café, the local meeting place for all of Shadeys upper crust, had given much attention to the old hermit Delbert Mucks, since he was dead and buried.

No Indian would go near where a body died – some Indians around Shadey said their spirit was still there – if they were evil – when they were alive!

As far as anyone knew, or cared, Delbert Mucks, if that was his name, was just the old hermit that used to live out in the woods. That was that! No one seemed to have even the slightest interest in who Mucks was, where he came from, or even his reason for existence – Mucks just existed maybe a figment of Shadeys short term memory!

Maybe Muck's had always existed at least in the memory of some of Shadeys Indian citizens.

For years, about every month or so, sometimes two or three, old Delbert would push his rickety, homemade, wheelbarrow, the mile or so into town. He'd go into Bruce Adam's Mercantile, buy some canned goods, some notebook paper, and some corn feed, load his wheelbarrow, and then mosey down to the post office.

Outside of catching the eyes of the locals, on his trips in and out of town, old Mucks went back out of sight, out of mind, and out of existence, until sometime later. The same old routine never changed nor did anyone in Shadey expect Mucks habits to change, until he came up dead.

## *Ch. 4 The Stranger*

It was a nice spring day. The Constable, Buford Nitch, Mayor Jim Bohannen, and Councilmen Otto Shorts and Bruce Adams were in their unofficial, monthly Shadey business meeting, setting at a table down at Mona's Café. Old Harley Fritzs had taken a seat nearby, in ear spot. Everyone in Mona's café took note when a well-dressed stranger came through the door.

As chance would have it, the only vacant table was next to the city fathers. The stranger, wearing a suit and a tie, in the middle of a work week, in Mona's Café, demanded lots of attention.

The stranger ordered breakfast and coffee, opened his briefcase, got a book out and began to read while waiting for his breakfast.

"Must me selling something" whispered Otto Shorts to the men setting around their table.

"Ain't nobody around here got enough money to buy an old setting hen" whispered the mayor.

Now a well-dressed stranger showing up in a Shadey was rather unusual. Such unusual occurrences always generated considerable attention.

The stranger, leisurely ate his meal, occasionally turning the pages of his book. The stranger was still engrossed in his book when Mona came to warm up his coffee and present the check.

"You're new around here" said Mona smiling, making small talk, while warming up his coffee.

"Uh, yes ma'am" said the stranger, putting down his book. "I hope I'm in the right town. I didn't see no signs as I came in. I'm not sure where I'm at, I hope this is Shadey. This is a long way from my home back east."

"This is Shadey alright," said Mona. "What brings you to our fair town?"

After a short pause, the stranger asks, "By chance would you happen to know where a Delbert Mucks resides?"

At the mentioning of Delbert Mucks, a stunned Mona missed the stranger's coffee cup and spilled a few drops of coffee on his book.

"Oh I'm so sorry" said the startled Mona, "I'm so sorry" sputtered Mona cleaning up the spill and drying the stranger's book. "Did you say Delbert Mucks?"

"Uh, yes ma'am – Delbert Mucks, I've heard he lives near Shadey," said the stranger, "This is Shadey isn't it?"

With Mona spilling coffee apologizing loudly, and with the mentioning of Delbert Mucks, you could have heard a pin drop! Everyone in the tables near the stranger was now all ears, while staring at the stranger.

"Yes sir, this is Shadey – all right," said wide eyed Mona. "Do you mean that old hermit that lived out by the river? You know him" asked a startled Mona, "you know him?"

"Not in person anymore" said the stranger now smiling, "but I'm very familiar with Muck's pioneering works, I'd really like to meet him, since I'm in the area. I don't get out in the field much anymore. I've not seen Mucks in years."

"You mean you want to see old Delbert Mucks" asked wide eyed Mona – "Delbert Mucks"

"Oh yes, in ornithology circles, Dr. Mucks, and his research is well known. This is one of his books" said the stranger, pointing at the now dry book lying on the table.

"Well" said Mona, having mopped up the spilled coffee. "There was a Delbert Mucks, if that was his name, that used to live out by the river, but I don't think he was known for anything, at least, not around here."

"The Delbert Mucks I'm looking for is well known in ornithology circles – worldwide," said the stranger. "I'd certainly like to talk to him, – it would be a real pleasure for me just to see him again. Can you tell me where I might find him?"

"The Mucks we know around here lived in an old shack out in the trees, a little way north of the cemetery, on the west side of the road, – but he ain't out there no more. He's buried out in the cemetery," said Mona looking intently at the stranger. "You kin or something to old Delbert?"

"Oh no" said the stranger obliviously disappointed, "Delbert was a giant in ornithology, a man like that will certainly be missed. That man was someone I'd certainly like to see again and talked shop with."

"Mr. – S – Sir" Stammered Mona, wide eyed, "What is that or – ornith – you know that word you call Mucks? Is that a ghost or something? – I ain't never heard no word like that before."

"Or-nith-ology" said the stranger, slowly smiling, "Ornithology – the study of birds – Dr. Mucks was a Corvusologist – a recognized authority on crows. His research with crows set standards in animal behavior science over the many years of his research; his contributions will certainly be missed."

The stranger was taking to his feet, about to pay his check and leave Mona's Café, when Buford Nitch jumped to his feet and confronted the stranger.

"Sir – a – sir" Stammered Buford, "I'm – I'm Buford Nitch – the law around Shadey – I'd really like to talk to you for a moment. – We couldn't help but hear your inquiries about old Delbert Mucks. I'd – I'd like – we'd like to talk to you – if we could. The Mucks out by the river have been dead a year or so – no one around Shadey knowed much about Mucks – he just stayed to himself."

"I see," said the stranger.

"Anyway" – said Buford – this is Jim Bohannen, Shadeys mayor, and this is Otto Shorts and Bruce Adams our Councilmen, and that guy standing is Harley Fritzs, he's – he's Harley Fritzs. What brings you out to our neck of the woods' we didn't catch your name?"

"I was an ornithology representative at the ornithology symposium up at the University in Ada. We were discussing Muck's research, among other things. I was in the area, I thought I'd try to see Dr. Mucks again – it's too bad I'm too late – you said your Delbert Mucks died a year or so ago?" ask the stranger.

A year or so ago, affirmed Buford.

"Hum" mused the stranger, "You say Mucks died a year or so ago?"

"Yes'um a year or so ago," affirmed Buford. "I investigated his death."

"That's odd," said the stranger. "We got his latest research paper not a month ago. Most of our contacts with Dr. Mucks, by his insistence, was with his assistant – I can't recall her name – right off hand – might have been – maybe Molly. Mucks said she lived around here somewhere, too."

"This Delbert Mucks you're talking about was he from Shadey?" asked Buford. "That Mucks out by the river – now there was an odd duck – if ever I saw one."

"His correspondences were always post marked Shadey Oklahoma," said the stranger. "We just assumed this is where he did his research. – It had to be a remote area."

"There were lots of crows out around that old shack. It was well into the woods – it was like – like- some of those birds out there – they didn't act like regular crows – it was like - like crows could talk!" Confessed Buford. "Real crows don't swarm you like a bunch of bees either. Them Crows, out at Mucks place, came right after me!"

"Crows can talk," said the stranger smiling. "Mucks research had to do with learned animal behaviors. Crows have about the same cognitive capacity as monkeys. In short – what you could teach a monkey to do you could teach a crow – according to Mucks book – with patience, crows could learn conditional responses, too, – you know, tricks too."

"Now and then" said Buford, "I hear complaints of crow attacks on humans – they peck'um on back of their heads – is that possible?"

"Aggressive behavior, in animals or men, can certainly be taught, however, that behavior may just be instinctive. Crows have been known to be extremely protective of their sources of food and their territory. Crows don't bite the hand that feeds them – like some humans. Mucks work with crows is well documented – that is what this book, by Delbert Mucks, is all about," said the stranger holding up the book in his hand.

The city fathers, sitting around the table were hanging onto every word the well-dressed man said. At last Harley Fritzs couldn't stand it no more. Jumping to his feet – he butted in – "Several crows around here, seem to talk all the time – is that possible? - I even got whooped on my head twice – I thought it was Mucks Ghost that done it!"

"Delbert Mucks' wasn't no ghost," said the stranger smiling. "At least, not the man that did the research and wrote this book. He wasn't a ghost."

"Well it was something evil" said Harley. "I's minding my own business!"

"I see" said the stranger, - "Corvusdiaes like crows – that were taught words and learned behaviors, according to this book, have been able to teach other crows their learned behavior, - to the third generation – that was groundbreaking research!"

"Mucks did that?" said Buford.

"It would have taken years and years to develop a working relationship with those animals. Muck's many accomplishments were monumental – he'll be missed," said the stranger remorseful.

The men gazed at the stranger in stunned amazement as he paid his check and vanished out the door, got in his car and headed out of town.

## *Ch. 5 Another Look*

When the well-dressed stranger paid his bill, walked out the door of Mona's Café, got in his car, headed down the highway back out of town, there was an eerie quiet in Mona's Café. All the eyes in Mona's Café had seen the stranger. Mona and a good number of Shadeys citizens had heard the stranger explanation about talking crows, too.

"Did you hear that?" said Harley Fritzs, in disbelief, after the stranger had departed the premises. "I can't believe him saying crows could talk – and that Mucks of all people, was a somebody!"

"We heard what he said" said Jim shaking his head. I ain't to sure I believe all he said – but he sure didn't look like no riff raff. He talked like he knew what he was talking about."

"Saying it, don't make it so" said Otto. "Look around the table, saying crows could talk don't make that so either. That stranger saying Mucks, if that was his name, was a well-known somebody, in bird circles, don't make that so either." Looking confused, Otto asked, "How could Mucks be a somebody and nobody around here know it?"

"Well" said Harley, sarcastically, "Mucks didn't look like no doctor I ever saw, down at the clinic."

"Harley" said Buford, sharply, now setting back down, "They's another kind of doctors beside people doctors and horse doctors – doctors is somebody that knows an awful lot about something. They was a law doctor, up in school, back when I was a rooky in training."

"Well I ain't never heard of no doctor Mucks – has you'ns?" said Harley, looking about at his companions lost in reflective thought.

Silence set in. The men sat there silent in deep thought. When, at last, Mayor Jim Bohannen said, "Buford, maybe we need to have another look out at old Muck's place – maybe we missed something."

"What for?" said Buford. "They wasn't nothing left out there but trash – and a bunch of dammed talking crows."

"Maybe that is something" said Jim, after a thoughtful pause. Jim asked, - "Buford did I just hear you say you heard some crows talk out at Mucks?"

"I didn't know it was crows," said Buford. "I just thought I might be seeing and hearing things – maybe the wind."

Bruce Adams had set there quietly, listening to his companions' discussions – "What was that strangers name anyway?"

"I'm beginning to think old Delbert Mucks is a name I'm not likely to forget again, anytime soon." Otto said, shaking his head, then he asked, "Do you suppose that old recluse was that somebody that stranger was talking about?"

"It has to be," said Bruce. "Surely they ain't two Mucks in the whole world – besides, we've been overrun by crows lately. I was even beginning to think there might be something to all that gossip. I've been hearing about crows being Mucks ghost."

"Well I'd like to forget this whole damned mess, but I can't," said the mayor, Jim Bohannen. "Every time I turn around somebody's got a complaint about crows or ghost or something. Lately every time I've seen a crow, I've thought there's another Mucks ghost."

That afternoon, Buford, Jim, and Otto made their way back out to old Mucks shack for another look see.

"This place gives me a bad case of the willies," said Otto. "Look at all them crows up in that tree. Some of these Indians we got around here think crows are spirits of their dead ancestors."

"I've heard that," said Jim. "I never put much stock in it, - it's like some of them other superstitions them Indians got – and now, we got a country full of talking crows – according to that stranger. Who was he anyway?"

"Buford said he was a ghost that makes about as much sense as Mucks being a doctor and crows that talk," said Otto.

"You've seen those pictures I took," said Buford opening the door to Muck's shack. "That's where old Mucks was a laying.... everything looks like it did the last time I was out here when I finished my investigation."

"Where was that pile of papers you took pictures of?" asked Otto. "They might say something!"

"They was right over there in that corner" said a startled Buford, pointing – "they's gone now!"

"Somebody must'a thought they was important" said Otto, looking at the photo. – "What was in um?"

"Thay's just stuff – I didn't read all of it – it was mostly handwritten, something about nothing – that's all – wasn't nothing important. What I looked at, looked like what you'd save for kindling – something to start a fire in that old cook stove." said Buford. "It was just a stack of old scrap paper - that's all – nothing important – why anyone would want kindling paper is beyond me!"

"Well somebody must'a needed kindling" said Otto, looking at Buford's photographs. "That picture of that woman, hanging on the wall over Muck's bed, is gone too."

"That picture was still here the last time me and Buford was out here poking around," said Jim. "I took a real good gander at that woman's picture. Best I can remember that woman kinda looked like somebody I've seen before – a long time ago – it could almost be a young Molly Grubs – she was a real looker back then"

"You bet she was" said Otto smiling. "Half the young bucks in the county was after that young squaw – included me – uh – uh – uh – what a beauty – you know – for an old woman. She's still pretty well preserved of course, I's young back then!"

"Me too" said Jim, smiling. "Us farm boys just dream about such beauties – maybe we still do!"

"Buford, did you know Molly back then?" asked Otto.

"Nope" said Buford, "that was back before my time in Shadey. I've heard lots of talk about her, and her pappy since I've been constable around here."

"Molly just lives across the river in that old house over yonder, when she's here," Otto said, pointing across the river. "Maybe we orta go talk to her, if she's home."

"What for?" said Buford. "It's a forty-mile drive across the river to her house – and I ain't gonna swim the river. I'll corner her the next time her and that old dog comes to town."

The three men nosed around a little while longer, then headed back to town.

"Molly must have known old Mucks – after all they was neighbors since the Stone Age," said Otto. "Do you remember when Mucks showed up out there?"

"Not exactly – I's young back then" said Jim, "and back then I's occupied with other stuff."

"Me too," said Otto, "that was a long time ago."

"It don't seem that long ago, but I guess it is," said Jim smiling. "Old man Grubs kept that girl pretty close to home, until she took off. When she come back, several years later, after her papa died, she had that school age young'un with her. Indians don't talk much – some said that young'un was a nephew – anyway, that was talk. – Them Grubs was some kin to Harley's squaw – I've heard tell."

"I didn't know that" said Otto, "them Indians all looked the same to me – except Molly – uh – uh – uh."

Jim was still struggling with memories of many years past. "You know, now I think of it – maybe it was Harley that was kin to them Grubs. Maybe I'll ask Harley next time I see him."

"If you're through reminiscing, let's go back to Shadey," said Buford. "I'm sick of this place anyway."

A few days later, Jim and Otto were setting down at Mona's Café eating dinner when Harley Fritzs came in.

"Come join us" said Jim loudly. "We've been wanting to talk to you."

"What about" ask Harley frowning, "I ain't done nothing to nobody, and I don't know nothing worth telling."

"Now Harley" said Jim smirking, "that ain't exactly so – anybody around Shadey, that wants to know something, knows to ask you or maybe Mona – at least when Mona's in a good mood."

"Well I was in a good mood until I got over here around you old goats," said Mona, pouring coffee. "I'm just a way to busy right now, to listen to your insults."

After Mona left, Jim turned to Harley, now setting, "just in the sake of interest" said Jim, now looking at Harley. "Me and Otto was wondering how you was related to them Grubs across the river?"

"I ain't!" said Harley emphatically, "them was Buellas kin folks. I don't even like um – never did," said Harley forcefully. Then Harley added, "Well now Molly – she used to be all right – but them other Grubs they was all worms."

"Now Harley," said Jim kinda smiling, "sounds like we may of hit on a sore spot. Grub worms don't sound to cordial."

"They never was much good about most of them Grubs. That old man, he's most of the problem," said Harley. "That rascal was always running rough shop, over them women, over there across the river."

"Well I knowed that old man was a might ornery – back when I was young," said Otto.

"No account!" said Harley, "more than once he'd get pie-eyed on that happy juice he's brewing, then he'd up and whop Lular. She'd then come a squallering across the river, over to our house for me and Buella to put up with."

"Uh huh" said Jim, "The in laws can be a nuisance.

"That ain't the half of it," said Harley, obviously annoyed. A few days later that old Grub worm would sober up, and come a whimpering, over to my house, trying to get Lular to come back home – he'd always swear he never do it again – he'd swear the devil made him do it."

"Well that stuff was kinda potent - best I remember," said Otto, "course I's young back then"

"Me to" said Jim, "we's stupid back then too."

"Uh huh" said Otto, listening intently to Harley, trying to get his facts straight. "Then I take it, Lular Grubs and Buella was sisters? – That means Molly Grubs is your wife's niece – ain't that right?"

"Nope, that ain't right" said Harley, kinda smiling – "I thought you fellers knew, Buella, my wife, is Lular's daughter –

so's Molly. There was a couple of no-account boy Grub worms, Stink and Moses that hold up over there, too."

"I knowed one of them" said Otto, "You know how the Indians are when they get tanked up on fire water. Things just don't work out well."

"We know" said Jim, shaking his head, "they's git's kinda wild – best I recollect."

"You bet they would" piped up Otto, "I knowed Stink Grubs. He's kinda homely. – Stink was pretty particular who tried to run with Molly. – I thought about shooting him a time or two – back when we was young."

"You mean you know Stink and Molly back then?" ask Harley, surprised.

"Oh yea" said Otto. "Nobody was surprised when Stink got drunk and shot over at Reachery – whatever happened to that woman and that young'un them two had?"

"Oh that woman got sick and died of something – some sort of cancer – we heard" said Harley. "Anyway, Molly wound up with Stinks young'un – Jimbo. Molly was back east some place in school or something when it happened."

"Some of us, around here, years ago, thought that young'un might be Molly's," said Jim.

"Nope" said Harley, "Jimbo was Stink's kid, Molly took him and raised him."

"I didn't know that." Said Otto, "I lost track of them Grub's after Molly left the county – it broke my heart" said Otto, smiling.

"We ain't seen or heard tell of Jimbo in years – at least I ain't." said Harley

"Where'd Molly go?" ask Otto. "That's about the time I went off to war – I never heard."

"Lular finally had enough, she quit the Grubs wormy and went off to that boy of her's back east and took Molly with her. After the Grub worm died, Molly and the kid wound up with the home place – nobody else wanted it – it wasn't good for nothing no how – we thought. All of them other Grubs was looking for greener pastures. When Molly come back after schooling, she brung that young'un with her, set up housekeeping in the old place, and sold that place across the river to Mucks – that's how they got tangled up."

"Then you knowed old Delbert Mucks too, - way back younder" said Jim surprised.

"Oh I knowed him - didn't like him. He's a way to snooty to suit me" said Harley. "Molly got that way too – after she got schooled and started playing patsy – watsy with Delbert – that done it! I's done with both of them! So's Buella – we see'd to that!"

"Don't Buella and Molly talk anymore?" ask Jim.

"I guess they buried the hatched years ago," – said Harley. "When I'm gone, they chit chat some – when I was around they'd jabber in Indian. When they talked 'Mohican' I didn't know half what they was jabbering about anyway."

"Harley" said Otto, grinning, "that's a woman thing. You ain't supposed to know nothing, they don't tell you – ain't that right?" said Otto to Mona ease dropping on Harley's explanations.

"How'd you like getting throwed out of here?" ask Mona, smiling. "You'll know the meaning of that."

## *Ch. 6 Molly's Back*

By late July or August, the South Canadian River was usually down to a trickle. If you was brave, or stupid, and real adventurous, you could tippy toe, at a dead run, or swim in quick sand across the river.

The county road, if you wanted to call it that, ended at the river. A similar road terminated on the other side of the river. Eons ago there had been a wooden, one lane bridge that spanned the river, but it washed out sometime ago – about – the start of the second world war, so's it was said around Shadey.

Most everybody – at least the sit on the bank fisherman that had any sense, stayed out of the river. Besides, about a quarter mile east, the way the crow fly, was the railroad bridge. You could probably just walk the crossties, if the occasional train wasn't coming or you could drive thirty or forty miles and get to the other side. To make a long story short, not too many folks from Shadey had a reason to go across the river. All the land on both sides of the river was fenced and posted with no trespassing signs. The one exception was Molly Grubs.

Molly was known to walk the crossties occasionally. Molly's house was on the old Grub place across the river. She'd walk the riverbank on her property, walk the crossties and make it to the Shadey mercantile. She'd get a few items, put them in the saddle bags on her big dog's back, go to the post office, then head back down the track, cross the river and go home.

Back down the railroad, north, across the river, seven or eight miles was another isolated community called Reachery.

As a general rule, what happened in Reachery – stayed in Reachery – what happened in Shadey – stayed in Shadey, besides Reachery and Shadey, because of the south Canadian river, were in different worlds.

From local accounts, the old spinster, Molly Grubs, had lived in that old house across the river from old Delbert Muck's shack about as long as anyone in Shadey could remember. Sometimes it would be four or five months – maybe even a year – before she'd make her appearance back in Shadey. It was during one of those absences, when old Delbert Mucks probably died, sometime in the spring.

It was sometime in mid-August when Molly and old Soap, Molly's old pack dog, made another pilgrimage to Shadey. It was fairly early one morning when Molly was outside Bruce Adam's mercantile, when he opened up for business.

"My my, you're an early bird this morning, said Bruce smiling, "You ain't been around in a coon's age – is Soap getting fat?"

"Me and Soap has been back east, visiting and working" said Molly, somewhat subdued, "Soaps just been eating and laying around. We thought we'd get our buying done before it got to hot. You know how August is."

"It's been a scorcher this year' said Bruce, looking insistently at Molly. "Is there anything I can do for you?"

"Is the constable out and about?" ask Molly, with tears in her eyes.

"He ain't showed up yet, he's off a cattle rustling. You know how those city officers are - they work banker's hours – anything I can do?"

"I'll leave the constable a note," said Molly.

Molly, bought a few things, loaded old Soap, went to the post office and left Shadey. It was a year or so, maybe next August, before Bruce saw her again.

Old Delbert Mucks had been dead and buried at least a couple of years or so when a new car came into town. The last time a new car came into town was when the stranger came into Mona's Café and managed to get Shadey in an uproar, a year or so ago. The stranger had suggested, Delbert Mucks, Shadeys old recluse, that lived down by the river, was a somebody, and that Mucks ghost was probably responsible for Shadeys strange, acting, talking Crow population.

The new car motored down Main Street, out to the Shadey school house that was now closed, for some time. It came back into town then traveled out to the cemetery. A young man and an elderly, well dressed lady, walked around the cemetery, as if looking for a particular grave.

"Who do you suppose that is?" ask Harley to his wife, both standing at their kitchen window. After several minutes of intent scrutiny, "That woman kinda looks familiar."

After searching the cemetery, the couple went back to the car. They drove on down the road north, to Mucks driveway. The young man opened the gate, got back in the car, and headed into the canopy of trees, shading the seldom used lane. The last car that went down that lane was Buford's cop car, two years or so ago.

An hour or so later, the car emerged from the timber. The young man closed the gate and drove back to Shadey.

When the car headed into the old Mucks place, Harley took it upon himself, to report the prowlers to Buford. Buford was nowhere to be found.

Harley then made his way to the mercantile, to see the Councilman Bruce Adams, to report the intruders.

Harley Fritzs was about to leave the mercantile when the new car arrived in town and parked out front of Bruce's store. Molly got out, and entered the store, greeting the smiling Bruce Adams. Seeing Molly, Harley vanished to the storage room in back of the Mercantile and remained out of sight.

"We haven't seen you in a coon's age around Shadey," said Bruce smiling, - "I almost didn't recognize you – is old Soap still up and about?"

"Old Soap is just fine" said Molly smiling. "I gave him the day off."

"You don't look like you was walking, anyway," said Bruce grasping Molly's hand. "It so nice to see you again – we've missed seeing you and that old dog, of yours, - that's the only pack dog I ever saw or heard tell of."

"Indians used to have them all the time before white men showed up with horse," said Molly smiling. "I guess me and old Soap are relics of the distant past."

"And who might this young man be?" asked Bruce extending his hand.

"That's my Jimbo," said Molly smiling, "He's my chauffer, now days. He's come back for a little visit - maybe for an extended stay."

"You mean you're that scrawny little kid that used to walk the ties and come to school over here?" asked a surprised Bruce. "You grown some since last time I saw you – It's got to be at least fifteen years – maybe even more!"

"I guess I was kinda puny when I went to school here in Shadey." Said Jimbo smiling – "It's nice to see you again, - can I look around?"

"You bet, help yourself," said Bruce smiling. "The candy is still over there," said Bruce pointing.

After Jimbo walked off, Molly continued the howdy do's, "He finished high school back east – and went off to college. He just wanted to see what Shadey still looked like – if it hadn't been so hot, we'd walked the cross ties again for old time's sake – old Soap likes those outings."

"I'll bet he do," said Bruce smiling. "At least he good for something besides eating and laying around – ain't he getting pretty old?"

"I've had him about fifteen years. Delbert gave me old Soap when he was a puppy. Delbert said I needed a companion, when Jimbo went off to boarding school back east. – My job teaching kept me busy."

The young man came back to where Jim and Molly was catching up on old times.

"It's nice seeing you again," said Bruce. "You've age some since I last saw you. Molly was just telling me about a young man doing good. Has Shadey changed much since you've been gone?"

"Shadey's about the same" said Jimbo smiling. "Same as ever – except for the old school – it looks empty."

"It is" said Bruce, "Most of the grown folks moved off looking for jobs and greener pastures – bout all that's left is us old folks, and a few Indian kids."

"Mom said Mr. Mucks passed on – where'd they burry him – we couldn't find his grave. I owe that man," said Jimbo.

"Out by the east fence," said Bruce. "The city buried him – he didn't have no kin nobody knowed of."

"Maybe I'll put up a big marker or something, someday," said Jimbo. "I owe it to him."

"So do I." said Molly with moisture building in her eyes, - "So do I."

"Mr. Adams, you still got field corn," asked Jimbo. "I'll take a couple of sacks."

"You Bet" said Bruce "It's still out back, - you'ns got chickens over across the river?"

"Naw", said Jimbo smiling, "Mr. Mucks' crows are probably hungry – me and mom was thinking about continuing Mr. Mucks work – we owe it to him, - after all he did for us."

"I didn't know Mucks had done anything for anybody?" Said a surprised Bruce Adams. "He didn't talk much when he come to town."

"He was kinda private" said Jimbo - "I owe him."

After Molly and Jimbo had left the store and left town, Harley Fritzs now emerged from the shadows. Harley was ease dropping having hung onto every word Bruce was having with the new arrivals.

"What do you make of that?" asked Bruce. "It's nice to see a nice kid make good – what kinda work did Mucks do that needs continuing?"

"Mucks was just another white man stealing from the humans - as far as I am concerned," said Harley. "When Molly sold Mucks that place over there, - she sold him the mineral rights too – those gas wells over there made Mucks rich - at Molly and Buella expense! Now ain't that gratitude!"

"I ain't never heard none of this," said Bruce. "It kinda makes since now – Mucks was monkeying with them crows. That's what that stranger was talking about, wasn't it?"

"It figures" said Harley obviously distraught. "I knowed Muck's ghost would come back and haunt me – I got to go talk to Buella – them's her kin folks – Grub's has always ment trouble! They always was!"

With spring and warmer temperatures came an abundance of crows. The trees north of Shadey seemed to be overrun with them. And now a good number of Shadeys fisherman, had reported, down at Mona's Café, seeing some unusual "Attics and Didoes" performed by some crazy crows!

On one occasion, little Wolf and Bobby Davis swore they'd seen a crow light out by their minnow bucket, flop upside down - spread its wings and start hollering, "Please"

The locals down at Mona's Café gave some consideration to how much beer they had consumed that day.

<<>><<>><<>>

A few days later a similar stunt was seen out by the cemetery. When Effie Mims had sat her water bucket down, after watering the flowers on her mammas grave. "There was two of them aggressive crows that came at me!"

Effie came tearing through Buford's office door, with eyes the size of saucers, yelling, "That crow attack scared me to death – they lit right in front of me – flopped upside down, spread their wings and started pleading for mercy! I peed all over my self! You got to do something – Now!"

"What do you want me to do?" said Buford, trying to keep his composure in the seriousness of Effie complaint. "I got no authority over the crow population."

"Well, they're a public nuisance!" said Effie empathetically – "Everybody knows it – somebody got to do something – ain't nobody safe no more around Shadey!"

"Yess'um" said Buford, trying to keep a straight face. "I'll look into it."

"You do that" said Effie storming out of Bufford's office. "I'll see you do that! I got a brother-in-Law that just loves lost causes. He'll have a way to get rid of them nuisance crows!"

## *Ch. 7 Grub Worms*

Little Wolf and Bobby Davis, longtime residents, beer drinking buddies, and frequent visitors to the riverbanks, north of Shadey, had reported seeing, that morning a strange behavior of a Crow in Mona's Café.

Now the story as told, down at Mona's was that little Wolf had just finished baiting his hook with a minnow, when this crow came swooping down from a tree, lit by his feet, flopped upside down, spread its wings and started hollering, "please, please!"

For the skeptical patrons there was some speculatorations as to how much beer they had consumed. It wasn't until Effee Mims filed that formal complaint in Mayor Jim Bohannens office, that same day the crow story came to life!

Little Wolf, Bobby, a few cans of beer, and their fishing gear had walked the riverbank, upstream, to the little clearing, where the crow encounter took place. A few days earlier, on the south side of the river, in the clearing, a hundred yards or so south, was the old Mucks shack. At top of that big tree, was a considerable number of congregating crows. Little Wolf, being Indian, was somewhat apprehensive to be in the proximity of where old Delbert Mucks was found dead. According to little Wolf, with a wary eye, Muck's evil spirit might still be around. With that crow's behavior, - that confirmed it - that done it! Little Wolf was ready to go back to Shadey – Now!

North across the river a good way, but in plain sight, was the Grub house, – with that new car parked out front. Bobby, and little Wolf had both taken notice, that Molly and that young man, were seen working in the garden getting ready for the spring planting. It was soon common knowledge, around Shadey that the long time – sometime – resident of the Grubs place was back. That Jimbo, her nephew, was planning on a stay across the river.

Molly Grubs was, almost, a Shadey resident, even if she lived across the river, in a different county, and maybe in a different world. Shadey was the nearest community to the Grub's place across the south Canadian river. Molly would walk the crossties of the railroad bridge to do her shopping and her occasional daytime socializing over at Bruce Adams store. Some speculated Bruce Adams, the old widowed, had more than a casual interest in the old, well preserved spinster.

It soon became common knowledge, Molly Grubs, and her nephew Jimbo, were setting up their residence in that little old house on the north side of the south Canadian river.

Back in the prohibition days, old man Grubs had MANAGED a small fortune making and selling moonshine. So's it was rumored. He had bought several hundred acres of cheap Indian land, on both sides of the river. When the bridge washed out, half his business was confined to the north side of the river, - mostly in Reachery and a lot farther north and east. It was rumored in Shadey, that old man Grubs was selling his produce to some riff raff back east – maybe Chicago.

Back in the twenties and thirties, moon shining was a way poor folk in southeastern Oklahoma could make an honest living – in way out of the way places. There were several stills in the woods back then. It was also common knowledge, back then, if you wanted to live and do well, it was best to forget where a still was, who was running happy juice and where to stay away from.

Molly Grubs and her nephew Jimbo were setting up residence on the north side of the south Canadian River. Soon it was speculated, somebody was feeding them nuisance crows! Not only were the crows around Shadey heard talking, but on a regular interval, some dammed crow would catch some unexpecting person minding their own business and put a peck on back of their head!

When that stranger made his appearance in town, two years or so ago, and made that explanation in front of the city fathers, and numerous city residents, the Delbert Mucks stories took on a whole new identity. Mucks evil spirit, has captivated, then corrupted the Crows! It was time to take action!

When Jimbo and Molly had come to town, Buford Nitch, the towns constable, was in the college library up in Ada, trying to find out about Delbert Mucks, since Effie Mims, the irate Shadey School Superintendent had filed that complaint with the Shadey city council. Demanding action, Buford was encouraged to get to the bottom of Shadeys crow problem.

It wasn't that Buford had any great interest in birds – especially crows – that brought him to a college library. It was the city council, Effie Mims with her loud complaint, and the riddle of how a nobody, like Mucks, could be a somebody that wrote a book or books within a mile of Shadey – and no one knew it – unless Molly Grubs knew something. Some of Shadeys votes were demanding answers to surfacing questions.

In the college library in Ada, in short order, Buford found three books written by Delbert Mucks – and in the acknowledgements – there was a Molly Grubbs – and – Molly was identified as Delbert's assistant!

Now armed with his new information, Buford made his way back to Shadey, now resolved to run down Molly Grubbs and get some answers!

<<>><<>><<>>

It was late in the evening when Buford returned from Ada. – Harley Fritzs was pacing the floor in Buford's office.

"What's up" asked Buford, not particularly surprised, as Harley often frequented Buford's office.

"Molly Grubs and that nephew of hers are back in town" said Harley, obviously aggravated – "and they went out to the cemetery and then out to Mucks Shack!"

"That ain't nothing in either place for them to steal," said Buford.

"Well, they ain't got no business out there," said Harley, obviously annoyed. "And that young man, he's thinking about continuing Mucks work! I heard him!"

"What young man?" asked Buford, now interested "What works?"

"That crow stuff!" said Harley almost shouting, "Mucks was teaching them crows to steal stuff and attack people!"

"How do you know that?" asked Buford, now looking intently at Harley.

"Buella's got Mucks books – Molly gave'um to her after she found Mucks Dead – Mucks and Molly has been in cahoots for years. Mucks has been stealing from us Indians for years! – Molly's been in on it all along! It's in them books – I looked at um'!"

"Now Harley" said Buford, "I went up to Ada and hunted up them books Mucks wrote, - they ain't nothing, I saw, about stealing from Indians in them. It was stuff about teaching crows to talk and how to make'um do tricks!"

"Well one of them tricks Mucks was teaching crows was how to steal from Indians!" said Harley defiantly – "and Molly is in on it too!"

"Now Harley" said Buford, softly, shaking his head in unbelief, "I just don't see how teaching crows to talk is stealing from Indians. Maybe you need to explain that to me."

"Indians knowed about crows before any white man set foot around here. A white man – with Molly's help – is stealing our secrets!" Said Harley wide eyed.

"Now Harley" said Buford calmly, "I don't see how teaching crows to talk is secret stealing."

"Well there's more – Molly sold that place over there to that thief Mucks – and those mineral rights too! – Those gas wells over there on Muck's place orta belong to Buella – not some thieving white man!"

"What's Buella got to do with this?" ask Buford, shaking his head.

"When that old Grub worm, died, he left all that property to Molly and that kid" said Harley still aggravated.

"I don't see what Buella has to do with all this," said Buford, confused.

"I thought you knew," said Harley. "Buella and Molly are sisters."

"Uh huh" said Buford somewhat stunned. After a lengthy pause, Buford asks, "Did I hear you say Molly found Mucks dead?"

"I don't remember saying that," said Harley.

"Sounded like it to me," said Buford. "Maybe I'll ask Molly next time I see her; she seems to have lots of secrets."

"Molly's an Indian – Indians don't talk much," said Harley.

"I thought you was an Indian," said Buford.

"Just part," said Harley.

<<>><<>><<>>

It was a nice spring day when Molly and Old Soap walked the crossties of the railroad bridge and made a pilgrimage to Shadeys mercantile.

Buford was at Mona's Café with Jim Bohannen, Otto Shorts, and Bruce Adams having their weekly, unofficial, city council meeting. Buford was giving his detailed report of his findings up in the Ada library and his conversation with the irate Harley Fritzs. The meeting was about to adjourn when Mona, looking out of the not too busy café window, saw Molly and Old Soap go by.

"Molly's on her way to your place," said a smiling Mona. "I thought maybe you'd want to go see her."

At that, Bruce announced, "We're about done here" as he rushed out of the door of Mona's Café.

"I need to talk to that woman before she leaves town," said Buford, to Jim and Otto, both smiling, watching Bruce Adams run down the street after Molly.

When things settled back down, Buford continued: "According to those books I saw, up in Ada, a Molly Grubs was an able assistant to Delbert Mucks – either one of you fellers know anything about Muck's work or a lab?"

"All I know about Molly" said Otto, "is ancient history.... Back then, Molly was what hypocrites called a free spirit. It was about the time Stink got shot over in Reachery, that Molly just up and vanished – nobody on this side of the river knowed what happened to her. Six or seven maybe eight years later,

Molly showed up over there with that young'un. If anybody knew anything, I never heard it, of course by then, Rachel was keeping me occupied. Did you hear anything, Jim?"

"Naw, I guess I heard about the same stuff you did," said Jim. "The prettiest girl in the county just took off. That must have been some kind of ruckus that took place over across the river – the old woman, Lullar, and Molly took off back east. Some said about the same time Stink got shot, wasn't they another girl over there – maybe another boy?" asked Jim.

"Yeap" said Otto, "they was an older girl and an older boy - theys both gone from home when I's running with Stinky trying to court his sister, – uh – uh – uh – boy o boy was that Molly a looker – and one wild Indian – so was Stink!"

"I rode my horse over there one Sunday afternoon, hoping to see Molly, all them Grubs was gone except the old man. He's drunk as a skunk grabbed a shot gun and run me off. I never went back over there anymore."

"I wonder why?" offered Buford with one of his rare smiles.

"Maybe I can explain it" said Jim smiling.

"Anyway" said Otto smiling, "Molly was gone – it was ten or twelve years before I saw Molly again."

Then Jim continued, "Anyway I got wind that Harley Fritzs woman was kin to the Grubs – that was years ago. I used to do some haying down by the river, they was paying jobs, back then, for strong backs and weak minds. Old man Orr got hands where he could get'um – some of them Indians would make hands – some like Harley was no account – they's looking for the water bucket, quitting time, and Saturday payday."

"Well, you know what Harley said about them Grubs," said Otto. – "He's a saying Molly and Buella was sisters – they never looked like sisters, nor did they act like sisters – of course back then, Molly was all I was interested in – uh – uh – uh – was she ever a looker – she's still kinda well preserved for an old woman! Don't you think?"

"You better forget that" said Jim smiling, – "Before Rachel – you know – takes a club to you!"

"Oh, I made a point to keep Molly out of my conservations years ago," said Otto smiling. "It was a matter of self-preservations!"

<<>><<>><<>>

Buford, Otto, and Jim were still setting around a table down at Monas Café, mostly just talking. With Bruce's abrupt departure, the cities business, for the day was ended.

"Molly and Old Soap is heading back home" said Mona looking out the window. "Looks like Old Soap is loaded down... You know," amused Mona. "Maybe I need to get me a dog like that."

"Dogs don't wait on tables," pointed Otto grinning. "Crows might, if you'd be kind to um'.

"I'm kind to people and dogs, not dead beats," said Mona pouring another round of coffee.

I'm people so's Jim and Buford," said Otto harassing Mona, "you ain't very kind to us."

"Like I said" Mona replied walking away with her coffee urn in her hand. "I'm kind to people and dogs not dead beats."

When Mona announced Molly was leaving town, Buford hurried out the door to meet her.

"Miss Molly!" Hollered Buford, rushing outside to greet her. "You got a minute?"

"I've always got time for a handsome law man," said Molly, smiling that radiant smile. "What can I do for you?"

"Well," stammered Buford, now patting Old Soap. "I – I – don't know where to start?"

"Let's start at the beginning," said Molly, "I don't bite law men."

"It's – it's about Mucks" said Buford with difficulty. "I – I – was up in Ada the other day – in the college library – looking for Muck's books – they – they was three of um' – I take it, you must have known Mucks pretty well?"

"Nobody knew Delbert Mucks well," said Molly. "I just knew him for a lot of years – I met him back east - years ago – you know – at a happening – during the Vietnam War – back when he was young – at least I was."

"The books" said Buford, trying to regain his composure before Molly – "Birds, ah – crows - ravens- magpies..."

"Corvus" said Molly smiling her captivating smile. "Delbert really liked crows – crows was his life – they always were – he spent most of his adult life studying crows."

"And you helped him with his bird study?" asked Buford.

"It was my good fortune to help him, what I could – he was dedicated – delightful – charming – compassionate – and unassuming to be around – and helpful – "said Molly remembering. "I – we- -me and Jimbo owe him. Finding him dead was devastating to me as it was to Jimbo."

"Then you left me that note?" asked Buford, seeing a cloud coming to Molly's eyes.

"There didn't seem to be nothing else to do" said Molly, in a soft voice. "You were gone, and he'd been dead quiet sometime."

Molly's eyes, now clouded – "I should have been with him" said Molly, now brushing away the tears – "I should have been here, with him – not teaching a class to a bunch of bird enthusiasts."

"That stranger?" said Buford softly, "that came – did you know him too?"

"O" said Molly, "that was probably Doctor Evens. I worked for him several years ago, as a secretary when I was in college. He's another bird enthusiasts."

"This Dr. Evens, he seemed to be an admirer of Muck," said Buford stuttering. "How? – how - what- how'd they know one another?"

"When Delbert was working on his PHD, Evens was an under grad – he's now head of the Bird Department in Outland U. – That's where me and Jimbo went. We're birds of a feather," said Molly smiling.

"I see," said Buford smiling. "Birds of a feather? – Is that crows?

"Jimbo is the biologist. He wants to continue Delbert's work," said Molly, "Jimbo was always under Delbert's feet over at the lab, when he was a boy."

"What lab?" asked Buford stunned, "I didn't know there was a lab – all I saw was that shack and a couple of out buildings – and lots of crows!"

"Oh my" said Molly, "I thought you knew. Delbert's lab is about half a mile southwest of his retreat. The lab is buried up in that timber west of there."

"I'd like to see that lab sometime," said Buford.

"When you have the time, and up for a nice walk, to the enchanted forest, with a nice lady, I'll be glad to give you a guided tour," said Molly, now smiling that captivating smile. "It's within walking distance of Jimbo's house."

"There's no road on west of that shack" said Buford, now in deep thought. "You mean there's a lab back in that timber? When would be a good time to see it?"

"About anytime," said Molly. "Jimbo is over there about every day. I can meet you some morning, we'll take a nice stroll to the enchanted forest."

"I'd like that" said Buford, looking at Molly.

"It's getting late – me and Old Soap wants to get home before dark, - nice talking to you. We'll talk again, sometime soon," said Molly, now leading Old Soap towards the railroad.

Buford just stood there – watching as Molly and Old Soap walked north out of town making her way to the railroad bridge. It occurred to him; he had not made a date to see the lab.

Buford made his way back into Mona's Café, somewhat subdued. Jim and Otto were still there,

Buford sat down. Deep in thought with his conversation with Molly.

"Well," said Jim, "Did you get an ear full?"

"That's some kind of woman," said Buford. "I can tell you that."

"She always was," said Otto. "That smile – it – it makes you heart go pitter pat, don't it?"

"Uh huh" said Buford, "did you men know there was a lab in the timber, west of old Mucks shack? Molly called that shack Mucks retreat – she said that lab was within walking distance," said Buford, looking from Otto to Jim.

"Not that I know of," said Otto. "It's snaky out there by the river – I don't like snakes, chiggers or ticks, which timber down there is full of um."

"Me neither," said Jim. "All I knew about was them gas wells, on that oil lease. Them wells is all south. Ain't nothing I know of up north – that land is all posted anyway, with no trespassing signs and locked gates."

"Well, there must be something out there," said Buford. "Molly said that nephew of hers was over there about every day. How could there be a lab out there and us not know it?"

"That's simple," said Otto. "Nobody but Indians go prowling around where they ain't got no business - and they ain't talking to no white man."

## *Ch. 8 Molly*

Into everyone's life a little rain must fall. Recently in Buford's life it was raining buckets full.

Buford had heard crows talk and he had seen some unusual behavior when he was investigating Mucks death. Jim Bohannen, Shadeys Mayor, and Otto Shorts, a Councilman, had both heard ghosts out at Harley Fritzs place not long after Moses had dumped Muck's bones in the hole, out at the cemetery's east fence, and covered him up.

When, somehow, the word got around that Delbert Muck, a real somebody – a Shadey resident – had been unceremonially buried. Some suggestions had come to light in the mayor's office that Mucks was entitled to a memorial. It was also pointed out by some voters that maybe Mucks had been teaching those crows that unusual behavior.

Those pecks on back of several heads was a different matter, there was complaints. Some complaints' like Effie Mims, a voter with lots of influence, had filed a formal complaint down in the mayor's office. Rumors began to surface, out at Bruce Adams store, that a recall petition, sponsored by Effie Mims was threatened if something wasn't done about those crows!

Nothing in Buford's law schooling had prepared him for a crow revolt. He had been Shadeys law man over twenty years. Nothing like this had surfaced before, in Shadey, but now crows couldn't be ignored.

<<>><<>><<>>

Buford had been to the library up in Ada, he had looked at Mucks Books and had a fair idea what Mucks had been doing for the last thirty years, but it still left lots of unanswered questions. If anyone knew about Mucks, it had to be Molly Grubs.

Buford was beginning to think his world was spinning around Molly – and those damned crows. What was even more perplexing was the fact none of this came to light until someone, probably Molly, had left a note in his door announcing there was a dead body out at Mucks shack.

A body that had been dead and deteriorating for six months didn't leave much to investigate. Mucks, Shadeys old recluse, just existed, and probably died of old age or by the ravages of old age, there was no cause for concern – until – that unusual behavior of a bunch of damned crows crops up! After Mucks was removed and buried, Buford and the city officers had concluded their investigation nothing was amiss but a photograph, of a pretty woman and a pile of kindling paper stacked in a corner.

<<>><<>><<>>

Several days had passed since Buford had talked to Molly. He had failed to make a date with her so he could see the lab. In recent days, much had come to light, that he knew nothing about, despite the fact it was within his jurisdiction.

Buford had eagerly watched for Molly and Old Soap's return, but in the meantime the Mucks mystery just deepened.

It was a forty-mile drive, roundabout to the Grubs house across the river. He had seen the Grubs house, in the distance, on the two occasions he had been to Delbert's shack, while investigating his death three years ago.

Recently Buford had gone out to the lane that led up to the Muck's Shack. But now a new gate and a no trespassing sign, blocked his way.

Curiosity may kill cats, but it drives law men, like Buford, to a nagging aggravation. What appears so obvious with the discovery of Mucks body, was now a deepening obsession. How could Muck, a Shadey nobody, be a somebody – a real somebody – and the city officials not know it? After his short encounter with Molly, and his trip to the Ada college library, Buford was now, actually aware, his investigation, now demanded answers, and then – there was those damned crows.

<<>><<>><<>>

The call of Molly was upon him! It was a quiet day in Shadey. Buford had decided to take the long drive, some forty miles, to get to the Grubs house across the river. After getting to Reachery, Constable Buford Hitch, Shadeys law man, looked up James Dobbs, Reacherys constable, an old classmate from their police academy days. It had been years since the old acquaintances had seen each other.

"What brings you out, across the river, to my part of the world?" asked a smiling James. "It's been a long time no-see."

"A wild goose chase" said Buford, with a rare smile. "No – maybe that's a wild crow chase. I'm trying to run down a Molly

Grubs. She lives on your side of the river. You can't get to her place from over there, except swim quick sand."

"They ain't but one Molly Grubs in the world like our Molly Grubs," said James, smiling. "Everybody knows Molly. That's some kind of a woman. You after her now – or is she after you?"

"I just want to talk to her," said Buford. "She seems to have lots of secrets – about lots of things – even about crows. How do you get to her place from here?"

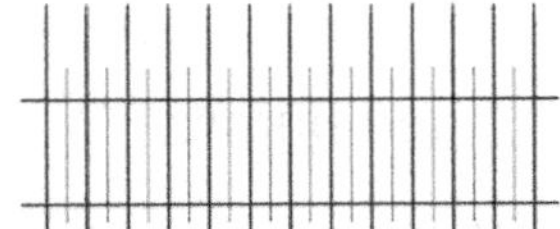

"Crows?" said James, grinning. "That woman could charm a cobra into a pussy cat, – that's no secret. Which place you looking for, her house on a hill or the one out on the river?"

"I didn't know she had but one place," said Buford.

"You don't get around much on my side of the river, do you?" said James. "You can't get over here, from over there. They ain't no bridge and it's a forty-mile drive, and I ain't walking no crossties."

"I guess we are kinda isolated. Quicksand discourages river wading," said James. "It's been at least ten years since I was over at Shadey.

"Well, I ain't never been to Reachery," said Buford. "You say Molly's got another place over here too?"

"Let's step out to the door - I'll point out Molly's place on the hill, on down the yellow brick road a ways, six or seven miles, is Crowville. You won't get lost – unless Molly puts a spell on you!" said James all smiles.

The two law men stood on the front step of Reachery City Hall; James pointed south toward a hill in the distance. "That's Molly's hangout, when she is in town, everything from here to the river belongs to her. That's the old Grubs estate, if she ain't there, she probably down on the river with that kid of hers. Molly said that kid was thinking of continuing Muck's work. That lab's on your side of the river. It's quite a place ain't it?" said James.

"I ain't never seen it," said Buford. "Molly said she'd give me a guided tour when I was up for a stroll."

"Lucky you" said James, grinning, "lucky you!"

<<>><<>><<>>

Buford made his way down the road aways to a closed gate – the gate opened upon its own! He came up the drive, parked his car, walked up the veranda to a kinda large door. He started to knock, but the door began to open on its own! When it opened there stood Molly.

"Well," "Well," said Molly smiling that radiant smile. "The handsome law man from Shadey has come a calling. James said you'd be along shortly."

"Uh yess'um" said Buford stammering, "I – I – I"

"Well spit it out" said Molly smiling. "I don't bite handsome law men."

"I – I don't know where to start," said Buford, looking at Molly. "I don't ....

"Seems we've had this conversation before," said Molly with that captivating smile, "Come in and sit a spell, we'll talk about it – I got coffee, tea, and bourbon."

"Co – coffee will be fine" said Buford with his hat in his hand, following Molly into.... a kitchen?

"Excuse the informality" said Molly, "I don't entertain vary often anymore, I'm more at home out on the river with the crows."

The maid took Buford's hat and poured the coffee, at the small table near the window with a view overlooking Reachery.

"What can I do for you?" ask Molly, looking intently at Buford.

"I – I just wanted to – to talk to you – that lab – you said – I'd like to see it – if I could – sometime," stuttered Buford. "I forgot to make an appointment."

"You up to a little stroll?" ask Molly. "Jimbo is out there – I guess. He's been busy lately – putting it back in shape. Jimbo's been staying out in the old place. Things got kinda run down since Delbert died – Lord we miss him!"

"This Delbert – nobody around Shadey seems to know anything about him," said Buford, now sipping his coffee and looking intently at Molly. "Harley Fritzs is about the only person in Shadey that even knew his name. He said Buella was your sister."

"That's Harleys' story – alright – said Molly smiling. "Lular, Buellas mama, was my papa's house keeper after my mama died. Buella and I were kinda raised together. We were like sisters – I guess, in the old days. Truth is, we're no kin. Harley always thought Lular should have some claim to papas place."

"Oh my" muttered Buford, "I don't know what to believe anymore."

"Oh" said Molly smiling, "There lots more – I'll tell you about it sometime."

"I don't want to pry into your personal affairs, but I have to ask," said Buford. "The young man, Jimbo, what's his connection to all this? Harley said he was Stinks' kid – who's Stink?"

"Stink was a nick name – his name was Reginal Sunsong. He was Buella and Neves youngest boy. He got drunk and got killed here in Reachery when I was in college at Outland – U. I'll tell you more about it sometime," said Molly smiling. "Oh Jimbo, he's my son – you up to a nice walk?"

"I was hoping to see that lab," said Buford. "The gate was closed with a no trespassing sign – I took a chance I could find you over here."

"I guess it's your lucky day," said Molly, with that captivating smile. "You found me – just loafing – I'll put my walking shoes on."

Buford and Molly got in Buford's car and headed down the dirt road, five or six miles, towards the river. They arrived at the old house and parked beside Jimbo's new car.

"The labs not far from here," said Molly, looking intently at Buford. "Maybe half a mile – across the river – can you swim?"

"Not very well," said Buford, concerned.

"Oh well" said Molly, seemingly disappointed. "It's such a nice day for a skinny dip – just a nice thought – anyway" said Molly, now giggling.

Molly led Buford down the well beaten path, through the timber, toward the river. After a pleasant stroll, and a pleasant conversation, they arrived at the river bank.

"Well – I'll be dammed" said Buford, showing surprise, standing there staring at the cable tram that spanned the river. "How long has this thing been here?"

"Since the thirties" said Molly enjoying the moment. "Papa built it when the bridge washed out, back before the war. Those several sections of land across the river used to be part of papa's place, too. Now it belongs to Delbert's son. Those are his gas wells too"

"I didn't know Mucks had any kin" said Buford, surprised – again. "I never heard of no son."

"Jimbo – he's Delbert's son" said Molly smiling.

"But – I – I – I thought you said Jimbo was your son?" said Buford stammering again.

"He is my son" said Molly smiling watching Buford's' confusion. "He's Delbert's son too."

"Then – then – you and Delbert were married," stammered Buford.

"Delbert was married to his work – not me. We liked it that way – he had his life's work – and I had mine," said Molly.

"Otto said you were a free spirit back then," said Buford, shaking his head.

"He orta know," said Molly, smiling. "He was kind of a pest for a while, till papa run him off."

"Oh my word," whispered Buford to himself.

After a while Buford was able to ask, "How do you work this thing?"

"There's room for two – if you stand real close" said Molly, smiling. "I'll close the gate – and you – the big strong lawman, can tug us across the river with that rope. I've not been this close to a real man in a long time," said Molly, softly.

"Yess'um" said Buford, pulling the cage across the river – "I – I ain't never done this before."

"It's real romantic after dark," said Molly, softly. "Oh well – just a thought – to bad you got a wife."

"Yess'um" said Buford, "I – I got a wife and kids too."

"So's I hear" said Molly, "Bruce is a wealth of information – I guess you know that."

"I used to think so," said Buford, tugging the tram across the river. "I'm not too sure anymore."

<<>><<>><<>>

Buford tugged himself and Molly across the river. Molly unlatched the gate and both stepped out of the tram onto the landing.

"Now what?" said Buford, securing the tram to the landing. "Where to now?"

"A skip and a hop that way," said Molly, pointing to a stand of dense vegetation and tall trees.

At last Buford asked, "Why is that lab buried up in trees?"

"Delbert's work demanded a natural habitat and seclusion," said Molly. "It takes a long time to gain a crows trust. Crows are weary of men, for good reasons. Delbert had to almost become a crow to gain their trust. That took years and years of dedication."

How'd he do that?" asked Buford.

"With patients," said Molly. "With lots and lots of patients – I never had the patients or the dedication Delbert had."

"But you helped him," said Buford. "His books said so."

"Oh I did what I could, when I could," said Molly with the shadow of tears appearing.

After a lengthy pause she said softly, "Sometimes he needed me – almost as much as he needed the crows – the crows were his life."

"I see," said Buford, seeing the pain in Molly eyes.

As they neared the stand of tall trees, Molly said, "Let's rest a few minutes."

Molly began to explain: "The crows – they know who they can trust, and are protective of their territory. They can be quite aggressive if they are being threatened. That is all spelled out in the books Delbert wrote."

"Maybe I'll do more than just look at some of the pictures next time," said Buford.

"I need to give you some instructions before we get to the lab," said Molly, now looking intently at Buford. "The crows are in charge over here – this is their domain – and you – a new comer – are intruding. They've not seen you before – except at Delbert's retreat. They will remember you – crows have a remarkable memory."

"I don't understand," said Buford, now looking intently at Molly. "I was only out there a couple times – a couple of years ago."

"They'll remember you," said Molly. "They communicate – exactly how, Delbert was trying to understand. Those crows will know you – or at least about you – they know you're coming."

"How do they know that?" asked wide eyed Buford.

"They know," said molly, smiling. "I don't know how they know – but they know. You hear that chattering in the tree tops in front of us? They know we're coming – the crows – they know we're coming – they are telling Jimbo."

"I –I – uh I wasn't hearing that chatter – I – I – I was watching – ah – paying attention to you – ah – at what you were saying," stuttered Buford.

They stood there – listening to the chatter in the trees before them. Then Molly advised Buford, "Soon – a crow – will appear behind you – if you move or flinch – he'll peck you! – If you stand still, he'll fly to the tree before us and lite."

Buford stood frozen to the ground – soon a crow passed within inches of Buford's head and lit in the tree before them.

"Stand still," said Molly, as the crow began to caw in the tree top before them. "He's deciding."

"What's he deciding" asked a somewhat shaky Buford with his eyes now transfixed on the crow. "What's? – ah what's he – deciding?"

"He's deciding if you can be trusted or not," said Molly, watching the crow – "we'll see."

After a few moments of deafening silence, Molly began to chime – "Hello!" – "Hello!" – "Molly!" – "Molly!" – "Hello!"

From the trees before them came "Hello!" – "Hello" – "Molly!" – "Molly!" – "Delbert!"

Molly answered back, "Molly!" – "Molly!" – "Hello!" – "Buford!" "Hello!" "Buford!"

"Bu! – By! – Buf! – Bufe! – "Buford! – Hello Buford!" said the crow in the tree top.

"Well I'll be dammed" said Buford, in utter amazement, his eyes still transfixed on the crow.

"Hello!" – "Dam Buford!" "Hello!" – "Hello!" – "Dam!" – "Dam!" – "Hello!" said the crow, as the crow took wings and flew south toward the lab.

Buford just stood there awe struck and speechless as the crow departed. "Well I'll be dammed," muttered Buford, "I'll be dammed."

"That's Albert" said Molly with that radiant – all knowing smile – now giggling at Buford's expression. "That's short for Einstein – don't you think?"

"I don't believe any of this," mumbled Buford, shaken his head in disbelief. "This just can't be happening!  I – I – I must be dreaming!"

"Albert takes a little getting used to," said Molly, grinning. "Wait until you met Alexandra – that's Alex the Great"

When Albert left, Molly and Buford continued on down the trail toward the lab.

"They'll be expecting us," said Molly, then she added, "Now don't be alarmed – they'll decide if your crow material or not – You've made a good first impression so far."

"You mean there's more?" asked Buford, concerned, staring intently at Molly.

"Oh yea," said Molly grinning, looking at Buford. "Soon – someone – probably Fred – will lite upon your shoulder – he'll nibble your ear – it's a little disconcerting at first – maybe even a little discomfortable at first, but don't panic – Its' crow behavior.  They're checking you out."

"Oh Lord," said wide eyed Buford, "This can't be happening!"

Soon, from somewhere, Fred lit on Molly's shoulder.  The crow looked at Molly, and then seemingly nibbled her ear.  The crow turned and espied Buford's ear.  Landing on his shoulder, Fred gently tasted Buford's ear, then flew into a tree nearby.

"Well I'll be dammed," said Buford shaking his head.  "I just don't believe any of this is happening!"

"So far so good," said Molly, smiling. "Maybe they'll accept you – with lots of patients, and perseverance – you might even make a crow – time will tell."

"Not in this lifetime," said Buford mastering a slight smile.

"That might be a long time," said Molly. "If the crows decide to accept you - you might find them useful – oh when we get back to my house, I'll give you Delbert's books."

"I'd appreciate that," said Buford. "I see I'm a child in Delbert's Land of Ozz."

# The Ghost of Delbert Mucks Part 2

## *Ch. 9 The Lab*

Molly and Buford continued them leisurely stroll toward the lab. Fred had taken wings and flew toward the treetops where a number of crows were chattering, and chattering, and chattering. Soon there was an eerie silence – the chattering subsided!

"What Happened?" asked Buford.

"Fred is reporting his findings," said Molly smiling. "Maybe you taste good – crows are extremely cautious - it will be quite some time – maybe years – before they will trust you."

"Why's that?" ask Buford.

"Delbert hypnotized, it has to do with crows survival instincts," said Molly. I've been making this pilgrimage over here for thirty years – the crows are still deciding my fate. It seems my erratic behavior is suspect – as is Jimbo's – I've had several long absences over the years. It takes a while – a long while to regain their confidence. Some of the crows – somehow – remember Jimbo as a child. It's been nearly twenty years since he was a resident here."

"I didn't know crows lived that long," said Buford, looking toward the treetops.

"Ordinarily, they don't. In the wild, some will live seven or eight years. There have been reports of crows living up to thirty years in captivity – that's a real rarity." Said Molly. "But somehow they keep an awareness of the past threatening encounters that's how they knew about you. You didn't threaten them.

"We're almost there," said Molly, as the two neared the small overgrown path.

<<>><<>><<>>

Nestled among, and amidst, the dense vegetation was the lab, - A rather large structure woven among the tall trees.

"How in the world did this – ah – structure come to being – in this location?" Said a startled Buford.

"All this is Delbert's handiwork over a long period of time." Said Molly. "He built what he needed when he needed it. The supplies were transported across the river, one bundle at a time – in full view, and consent, of the few resident crows, - this multitude you now see are mostly, second third and fourth generation of Delbert's patient, dedicated efforts."

"I've never seen anything like this" said Buford, "Is this where Delbert did his research?"

"Mostly, he lived here amongst the crows – in time, the crows began to except and trust him. Animal research has to begin with trust, - in short Delbert almost became a crow, - it took years to develop that close relationship." Confessed Molly, then she added, "His research – it was momental."

"How come no one around Shadey knew of his research?" ask Buford. "No one I ran across even knew his name – except Harley. All Harley ever had to say was something about Delbert stealing secrets from the Indians."

“That sounds like Harley,” said Molly smiling. “Delbert stayed away from Shadey and its people, like Harley, mostly out of necessity. Crows don’t trust people – for good reasons. You’ve heard of scare crows – not scare robins – crows know that. Delbert was able to overcome that distrust – that’s what made his work so special. In time, the crows shared their lives and their secrets with Delbert – it’s in his books.”

Buford and Molly were now in the lab. Buford was paying attentions to what he was seeing when Molly said, “Jimbo must be up with the crows some place – I’ll call him.” Molly hollered loudly, “Caw – Caw.”

From somewhere up above came a “Caw-Caw.”

“He’ll be down soon,” said Molly. “He’s in the crow’s nest, listening to the crow chatter.”

Molly and Buford walked past several cubicles toward a ladder ascending through a hole in the roof near the trunk of a tree growing through the structure.

Soon the young man appeared descending the ladder. “We’ve been expecting you” said Jimbo extending his hand toward the constable. “You must be the Buford, Fred talked about – I’m Jimbo – Mucks. I hear this is your first visit to the lab. The jest I get, the crows knew you from somewhere. We don’t receive many visitors.”

“I didn’t know this place even existed two weeks ago” said Buford shaking Jimbos hand – “I’m not to sure I believed what I see. Molly offered to give me a guided tour.”

"It does kinda take your breath away – a first visit," said Jimbo. "The crows like it that way. They are warrie of me! I've been around crows, one way or another, most of my life. Some of these animals still remember me, somehow, even as young as I was. They are congregating, expecting to see Delbert."

"Delbert is dead," said Buford, "matter of fact, don't they know that?"

"They know, but they are expecting his return," said Jimbo. "Exactly how, or why, or in what form is beyond me – but the crows say it will happen. With the aid of dad's research, maybe Delbert will return. Anyway, the crows are expecting him."

"Oh Lord," Buford thought to himself. "How can there be another ghost of Delbert Mucks?"

<<>><<>><<>>

The lab consisted of a number of cubicles, each designed for some sort of a test for the selected crow. The tests as explained by Jimbo and Molly were designed to gain an insight to the crows' cognitive abilities. Delbert had devised ways to study crows learning, memory, and problem-solving capabilities. Recently, according to Molly and Jimbo, Delbert had devised ways to study crows' speech and information transfer to their offspring. Delbert left his last discoveries, unpublished, in a pile in his retreat.

As the three walked through the complex, a number of the resident crows seemed to take considerable interest in Buford. A number of the older residents' crows made obvious references to Buford as Delbert.

"Molly – Jimbo – Buford," chimed Molly. The crows answered, "Molly – Jimbo – Delbert."

"Buford" corrected Molly, "Bu – for – ed." At last came "Buford" from somewhere.

Molly explained, "Some words are more difficult to grasp than others. Especially new words, Fred has spread the word Buford – you're now in the catalog of crow words – time will tell what Buford means in crow. You may become a celebrity," said Molly smiling. "How crows retain and pass on new words is not thoroughly understood, - we just know that they have been able to pass along information from one to another for three generations. That was a monumental discovery Delbert made."

As they continued their walk through the lab, a crow landed at Jimbo's feet, turned upside down and began to beg, "Please – Please."

Jimbo retrieved a treat from his pocket, showing it to the bird – "now beg."

The crow right sided up, lowered its head, "please – please" it begged.

Jimbo gave the bird a treat – "Alex can you sing for Buford?"

The bird now took flight, lit on Buford's shoulder and began to crow – "damn Buford damn – damn Buford damn – damn….."

"That's enough, said Jimbo, giving the bird a treat – "Alex – can you show Buford the latest dance steps?"

The crow now lit on the countertop nearby and began to prance, shaking its tail feathers in a controlled fashion. "Please" then came another plea from Alex. With another treat, the crow took wings and left the lab.

"That," said Molly smiling, "is Alexander the Great, his complete repertoire of tricks took Alex about nine years to learn. He has taught several of his offspring some of his tricks, - the 'please' you must have seen before – someplace. Alex remembers you."

"I have" said Buford, "out at Muck's retreat, during my investigation three years ago, there was half a dozen beggars flopped upside down. I've seen crows all my life. I never dreamed they could do such stuff, I...... I....... I just don't know what to say," said Buford after seeing Alex's performance."

"Alex can do other tricks too," said Molly smiling. "When he's a mind to – he's a little contrary sometimes. Alex has a daughter 'Cleo' that has the same capabilities as Alex. She's out someplace – courting, I guess. She's still a little shy around men she don't know."

"Smart girl," observed Buford.

<<>><<>><<>>

After a couple of hours of explanations and observations Molly and Buford headed back toward the tram.

"How can I explain what I've just seen?" ask Buford shaking his head.

"You can't," said Molly smiling. "My advice don't try. Most folks will think your nuts if you try to explain animal behavior. Even seeing is not believing, so's I hear around Shadey."

"You're right about that, nobody I know, in Shadey, would believe this," said Buford.

"That's why Delbert went to great pains to remain aloof from the folks in Shadey – for the crows benefit. Only a few – a very few on Reachery side of the river are aware of this work. – That's why there are locked gates and no trespassing signs on both sides of the river. Delbert needed the isolation," said Molly, now with tears in her eyes. "The crows, for good reasons, don't trust men – especially men with shotguns!"

It was well into the afternoon when Molly and Buford left the lab. What Buford had seen and experienced was beyond belief. There were so many questions he wanted to ask, but just couldn't. Nothing in all his years of law enforcement had prepared him for the crow encounter, with Molly, or the reality of the lab.

After leaving Molly at her estate home, Buford decided to go see James Dobbs again.

<<>><<>><<>>

"Did the crows bite you?" ask James smiling. "Did you taste good?"

"Molly said only time would tell," said Buford smiling. "That's some kind of a place over there – I never expected anything like that – and Molly – what can I say?"

Molly – I can tell you – and that place over there – kinda leaves one speechless," said James. "Over here, we do our best to keep Delbert and his work under wraps. That river and its quicksand is a big help."

"I didn't even know that lab existed two weeks ago, until Molly mentioned it," said Buford subdued. "I don't think anyone on my side of the river know about that lab at all."

"What you don't think you know about, you don't talk about," said James smiling. "I got my first tour of that lab about twenty years ago. Delbert and Molly impressed upon me the need for anonymity. After seeing that place a time or two, I agreed with them! I've made a point of letting them be. As far as I'm concerned what happens at that lab, stays at that lab – except for the books Delbert and Molly wrote – everything else stays at the lab."

"I can sure see the need for that now," said Buford.

"I guess you've seen Delbert's books, haven't you?" asked James.

"Just recently," confessed Buford. "I went up to the college library in Ada, the other day, and looked them up. But now, I'll be reading them from cover to cover in just no time. Molly gave me Muck's books."

"Those books make interesting reading!" said James. "I don't see how any man could do what Delbert did. – As far as I'm concerned, Delbert Mucks was a great man – and I don't even like crows!"

"I don't like crow either," said Buford. "But now, I don't know what to think about Mucks or crows. I have nothing but respect for both now."

"Oh, by the way," said James smiling, "Now and then, some pertinent, unsolicited information can surface in our business un-expected. It's only been in the last two months or so that the official word came to Reachery City Hall that Delbert Mucks was dead."

"My word," exclaimed Buford in surprise – we buried Mucks three years ago!"

"The wheels of the crow Gods must turn slowly – I guess," said James smiling. "Anyway, our city council got a signed petition by most of the locals, when the word got around Mucks was dead. Our citizens, mostly whites, wants Mucks dug up and reburied in our city park here in Reachery, with a sizeable monument erected to Reacherys most illustrious citizen. I guess you've heard about that by now – haven't you?"

"No one in Shadey has been notified – that is – that I know of," said a stunned Buford. "We buried Mucks three years ago! Who – why – who can get away with digging up dead bodies? Who even wants to dig up a dead body?"

"Some attorney has filed the petition with the county and state authorities," said James, "About all that's left is a judge ruling and a court order – at least, that's what I hear from our mayor's office.

"Oh my" mused Buford, "the mayor, in Shadey, will be thrilled to hear about this. We got a good number of citizens that want to erect a memorial in Shadey."

## *Ch. 10 Revelation*

Some days it just don't pay to get out of bed. Today, for Buford was well on its way to being one of those days.

For starters, it's just not every day, you find yourself caged up in an old cable tram, you didn't know even existed, with a tantalizing old cougar breathing on the back of your neck, while you're tugging on a rope, pulling the tram across a river. On top of that, that old cable tram was something you'd never seen, nor heard tell of, that was in your own back yard! And then – there's that sensation of having your ear nibbled on by a damned crow – how's about seeing, a grown man, roosting in a treetop – having a conversation with a bunch of damned birds, discussing your arrival?

Buford, now on his forty-mile drive, back to Shadey, alone with his thoughts about his full day of unusual, unforgettable, experiences on the river, in the lab, and later at Reachery taking with his old friend James, he's halfway expected the sky to start falling!

About sundown Buford arrived back in Shadey, wanting some peace and quiet, to reflect upon the day's activities - but – in his office was the Mayor Jim Bohannan, and the Cities Councilmen, Otto Shorts and Bruce Adams.

"Where in hell have you been all day?" demanded the Mayor Jim Bohannan, shaking a paper at Buford. "Look what I got – hand delivered – this morning – by one of those hack law clerks, that works for that jack ass judge – up in the city – delivered to the mayor's office – this morning!"

The sky – definitely was falling! There in the Mayor's hand was a court order – signed by District Court Judge Alvin Thomas – to exhume – the body of Delbert Mucks – for entombment in the Reachery City Park!

"Not only that!" said the irate mayor, "but I've had a reporter from the Gazette breathing down my neck, asking all kinds of questions about Muck and his work – like I was supposed to know all about it. Now, as late as it is, he's out in the cemetery nosing around, with that damned nuisance photographer that stood around snapping pictures!"

"How did some reporter get in on this?" ask Buford.

"It seems, according to that reporter, digging up dead bodies in Oklahoma is real news," said Jim. "It seems a dead body, in Oklahoma, has the right to stay buried. According to that reporter, digging up a dead body don't happen very often. Evidentially Muck had lots of clout with higher-ups some place, that thought he was somebody real important!

"I ain't never heard of them moving a dead body out of this county before – for any reason," observed Buford.

"Me neither" said Jim. "When I got that order this morning I made some calls. The jest I get, District Court Judge Alvin Thomas and Delbert Mucks were classmates in that university back east someplace eons ago. Some son of Mucks, supposedly, petitioned the court to have Muck dug up and moved to

Reachery – that was news to me – I didn't even know Mucks had a son- did you?"

"Not until this morning," said Buford. "That young man running around with Molly is Muck's son."

"How'd you know that?" asked Jim wide eyed.

Molly told me this morning," said Buford. "I went and hunted her up this morning – over in Reachery – and she gave me a personal tour of that lab, too. That's some kind of a place."

"I ain't never heard of no lab until recently," said Jim surprised. "You mean there is one?"

"Oh yeow" affirmed Buford, "there is one – and it's on the south side of the river – in that timber west of Muck's old shack – it's in our county."

"How'd you get across that river?" piped up Otto. "All I ever knowed about that timber, down by the river was tick, chiggers, snakes, and crows. You ride a tick or snake across the river or did a flock of crows fly you across?"

"Them ticks and snakes ain't big enough, and the crows were busy," said Buford smiling at Otto's caustic remark. "There's an old cable tram, that spans the river a little ways west of that house Molly and that kid of hers' lived in, when he went to school over here!"

"How'd that get there without us knowing it?" asked Otto.

Molly said her papa built that tram, after the bridge washed out before the war. All that property, for miles on both sides of the river belonged to her daddy, old man Grubs. Rumor has it he had business interest about where that lab is now."

"I'll bet I know what that business interest was a way back then," said Otto smiling. "They was lots of stills around back then."

"They may still be a few of them hooch factories around someplace," said Jim. "So's I hear, now and then."

"Well that house on the river ain't where Molly lived when I was chasing her," said Otto smiling. "She lived in that mansion atop that hill a couple of miles south of Reachery. Back then, my folks had a place over there outside of Reachery – my folks sold out and bought a place over here. When Stink was still alive, I'd ride my horse over there. That's how I met Molly. That whole bunch of Indians that lived in that house outback, in a matter of days, got shot, run off or just vanished, leaving old man Grubs all by himself, with his booze. Molly was gone when all that happened."

"That estate house is where I found Molly this morning," said Buford. "James Dobbs, the Constable over in Reachery is an old classmate of mine back in our police academy days. He filled me in on a bunch of ancient history about Mucks, Molly and old man Grubbs.

Molly was the only kid the old man had, but there was a whole tribe of Indians that lived over there, around the estate house, that belonged to his house keeper, Lular.

"I knowed there was a bunch of Indians, that lived back in another house, but I never knew their connection – Molly was, by far, the most interesting object of interest to me," said Otto smiling uh – uh- uh."

"With what James and Molly said – and reading between the lines," continued Buford – "it seems Harley Fritzs was after Molly too, back then, but he wound up with Lular's daughter, Buella instead. It seems Delbert Mucks arrived on the scene, handsome, rich, charming, and well educated. Old Harley just couldn't compete with all that – at least that's how I see it. If Mucks had a life, away from the crows, it was with Molly at that lab or in one of them houses over there."

"That explains a lot," said Bruce listening to Buford. "With what Harley has said over the years, and what little Molly has told me, the pieces fit together now – that explains that bad blood between Mucks and Harley that Harley was always harping around."

"Well, everybody around Shadey thought Mucks lived in that shack out west of the cemetery," said Otto, "at least I did."

"Me too," said the mayor. "I never dreamed he had a life someplace – maybe across the river."

"I didn't care where he lived," said Bruce quietly. "All I ever knew about Mucks was he was a cash paying costumer – always with ten dollar bills – I wondered about that sometimes."

"According to Molly," said Buford, "That old shack was Delbert's retreat from the crows. That's where he kept his notes and wrote his research papers and books. His latest research was that pile of papers."

"So's that's what that big pile of kindling paper in the corner was," said Otto surprised.

"Must have been, said Buford. "I guess Molly or Jimbo, that kid of hers, carried off those papers and has them now. One of them probably wrote that 'recent report' that stranger, down at Mona's was talking about, two years or so ago. After what I saw at that lab, that stuff would have been real important to them," by the way when's that dig supposed to take place?"

"A week from Friday, said the Mayor Jim. "According to that court order, our funeral home and undertaker is supposed to be in charge of the dig and transportation of the body to Reachery"

"Well now," mused Buford now looking intently at Mayor and councilmen, "that may cause us a little problem – we ain't got no funeral home or undertaker in Shadey."

"The nearest we got to an undertaker is Moses," said Otto. "He been in on most of the burying around here for a long time – epically for the Indians and the no accounts this city has to bury that washed up out by the railroad bridge. Maybe we orta get Moses to go dig up Mucks, put him in a box, and have him take what's left of the body to Reachery."

"Moses ain't got no truck and as far as I know, he can't drive," said Bruce.

"How's about little Wolf and Bobby Davis?" asked Jim. "Bobbies got an old truck – Buford could let'um out of jail – if they'd be willing to help Moses get the job done – they'll be sober in a day or two."

"Oh I don't know about them being sober," said Otto smiling. "They might do better drunk. If I's digging up dead bodies, I'd have to be drunk."

"You got Moses down there too?" asked Jim.

"No" said Buford, "But I can run him down someplace – we got a week or so – I'll see what I can find out about moving dead bodies – if Mucks was so important, maybe we orta keep him here."

"Oh I don't know about that," said the mayor. "We've had to deal with that damn judge in the past with him meddling in our city's business."

## *Ch. 11 The Dig*

Bright and early the next Friday morning, Buford went out to the old shack where Moses and his woman live.

"Is Moses around?" ask Buford. "I told him I had a job for him."

"Him gone," said Snow Bird.

"Where's he at?" asked Buford. "I need him. He drunk some place?"

"Him no come home. Me shoot'em. Him bad medicine, go

that way," said Snow Bird pointing north.

Asking around Shadey, no one had seen Moses in a week or maybe two. Even down at the gas station, where they sold beer – and spirits – out the back, Gus hadn't seen him.

"Maybe the earth swallowed him," said Gus. "Moses is one of my best customers – I shore does miss him.

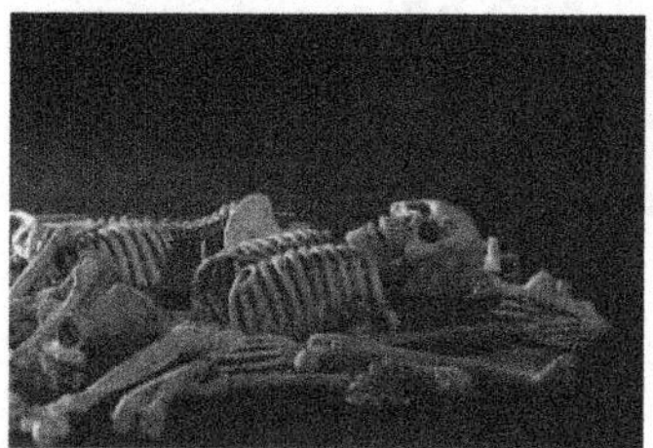

"You don't have no idea what happened to him?" Asked Buford. "I got a paying job for him."

"Last time he come in, he bought several bottles of – alt – you know – six pack of beer." said Gus smiling. "I asked him where was the party? He said out at the cemetery. That's all I know – ain't seen him since. - Uh- Rufus, was saying that was an Indian shin dig out at the cemetery the other night – I guess you know about that?"

"I've heard it mentioned," said Buford. "You wouldn't happen to know where I could find a little jug of that stuff you don't sell."

"I got a little jug of hooch – in town – the other day – at the liquor store. For my own use - you can have it – my women don't want it in the house – you know how cranky old woman are about such stuff," said Gus.

"I know – about that – but I got a sick horse that needs some doctoring," said Buford smiling.

"I didn't know you had a horse," said Gus smiling.

<<>><<>><<>>

After not finding Moses, Buford went by the jail to pick up Little Wolf and Bobby Davis – Both were hung over but sober.

"Would you fellers be interested in doing a little digging for the county – A couple of hours will take care of those fines you owe," said Buford, unlocking the cell door.

"Who died?" asked Bobby, "I ain't heard of no dying lately."

"Oh it's just a little digging," said Buford. "Ain't nothing to it – Moses buried something he wasn't supposed to – that's all. It's out at the cemetery."

"All I ever heard about old Moses burying was dead bodies and evil spirits," said Bobby.

"There ghost out there!" piped up Little Wolf, - "Lots of ghost – and crazy crows too!"

"It's daytime," said Buford. "You won't be out there any time – I'll be with you – if they's a ghost out there – I'll load my gun with silver bullets – that'll run'um off. Oh Bobby, does that truck of yours still run?"

"It did. It's down at Gus' place, out of gas," Gus said. He'd hold it until I got him paid off."

"Uh huh. How much is that?" Buford ask.

"Ten dollars" said Bobby.

"Uh huh," said Buford. "You suppose if the county stood good for that ten dollars, and filled your tank with gas, you suppose you could take a box over to Reachery? I'd even follow you to make Sure you got there and back, and show you where to take the box."

"That's a fur price," said Bobby.

"The county would probably pay twenty dollars for the wear and tear on your truck," said Buford. "Little Wolf can go with you."

"Is that twenty dollars cash," asked Bobby.

"I'll see that it's cash," said Buford. "You men get started. – Let's go get your truck."

The men got in Buford's car and went to get Bobby's truck. Oh – there a jug of 'smelling sauce' under the seat, - they say it's good for hangovers," said Buford.

After getting Bobby's truck and the diggers gassed up, Buford took them to Mona's and fed them – then over to Bruce's to load the box in Bobby's truck. "I'll meet you down at the cemetery in a few minutes," said Buford. "I'll show you where to dig."

"What we digging up out at the cemetery?" asked Little Wolf, concerned. "They's ghost out there – and crows too. Them crows is dead demons – that's come back to life."

"They won't bother you none I'll see to that," affirmed Buford.

Bruce Adams had gotten one of the handy men around Shadey to make a big pine box. It was down at the mercantile – there was a hammer and a hand few of nails on top.

"That'll do," said Buford. "You men put that box in Bobby's truck, I'll meet you down at the cemetery in a few minutes."

"Where's' Moses?" asked Bruce.

"Don't know," said Buford. "No bodies seem him in a week or so. He bought a bunch of spirits and told Gus he was going to a party – his woman said 'me shoot'um – that's all I know."

"You reckon he's laid out drunk some place?" asked Bruce.

"Most likely," said Buford. "You want to go see the show?"

"Can't right now," said Bruce. "Otto said he'd go – he's down there now – so's that reporter – with a photographer. Seems digging up bodies is real news – I hear they maybe a crowd down there."

<<>><<>><<>>

When Buford got to the cemetery, there were several people standing around Otto, by the front gate. Some looked like city dude reporters, photographers and nosy pokers – like Harley Fritzs.

Buford parked his car behind Bobby's truck – Bobby and Little Wolf – all eyes and ears – were just sitting there watching the commotion.

Harley Fritzs was standing among the strangers, listening to Otto, in the middle of the reporters, trying to answer and ignore their questions.

"There's the constable – maybe he knows something," said Otto in desperation. "I don't know where the grave is, I wasn't here for the burying."

In short order, Buford found himself the center of attraction, swarmed by men with note pads and cameras.

"Where is the grave?" yelled a reporter. "We can't find no marker – Muck's was a famous man – where's the grave?"

"You men stand back!" commanded Buford. "We got a job to do, right now I need to talk to that man," said Buford, pointing at Harley.

"Harley," said Buford, "I need you to show me exactly where they buried Mucks."

"It's was right over yonder by that east fence – where that mound of dirt is – but, Mucks probably ain't there no more," offered Harley sort of smiling.

"What in hell do you mean he ain't there?" demanded, a now irate Buford.

"Devils like Muck don't stay in graves very long – everybody knows that" said Harley. "At least the Indians do. If Moses hadn't been so drunk and done a better job of dancing when he buried Mucks, we wouldn't be having this trouble now, and the Indians wouldn't be mad."

"What in the hell are you talking about?" demanded Buford. "Dead is dead! – Buried is buried! – and I ain't no damned superstitious Indian!"

"You'll see" said Harley smiling. "The Indians know what will happen if you dig up Mucks and unloose the evil spirits. Mucks ghost will be out of the grave, looking for a new body."

"That the damndest stuff I've ever heard," said Buford looking at Harley.

"There was a powwow out here the other night, during that last full moon. All the local Indians got tired of all those evil crows attacking people and disturbing the spirits, they danced Mucks out of the spirit world and doomed it forever – to keep it away from the Indians. They made that mound to keep the spirit of Mucks – forever dead!" said Harley loudly.

"I don't believe any of this!" said Buford walking away.

Several of the reporters, standing around were ease dropping Harley's and Buford's conversation.

Near the fence on the east side of the cemetery, that was set aside for burying bodies at cities expenses, was a tall oak tree. With the ongoing commotion taking place near the cemetery's front gate, a number of crows began to congregate in the trees nearby.

After the conversation with Harley, Buford ordered, "you men stand back – there's work to be done!"

Little Wolf and Bobby followed Buford, carrying the pine box across the cemetery to the mound of dirt Harley Fritzs had pointed to.

As Buford neared the tree across the fence from the grave, a chorus "hellos, Delbert and Buford", greeted the men from the sky.

"See! I told you!" said Little Wolf, now with terror in his eyes. "I told you there was ghosts and demons out here! See! There they are" as he pointed toward the tree.

"It ain't nothing to worry about," reassured Buford. "It's just a bunch of old black birds with nothing to do but sit up there and chatter."

"They're evil!" yelled Little Wolf, "see I told you!"

"There just old birds that was taught to talk – that's all – they ain't going to bother you – I'll see to that," said Buford. "Now, let's get to work so we can get done and go home."

After Buford's assurance, Little Wolf and Bobby, reluctantly, toted the box to the grave site, all the time keeping an eye on the crows in top of the tree.

Buford looked up toward the crows – "well hello there."

In the tree top, in ears shot of the congregation sown at the front gate came a chorus of "Hello's."

"Hello – hello," "Buford" "hello," said Buford loudly.

From the tree top came a chorus of "hello" – "hello" – "Delbert" – "hello."

"Hello" – "Hello" – "Buford," "hello" answered Buford to the stunned amazement of Little Wolf, Bobby – and the congregation down by the front gate. Now several cameras were pointed toward Buford.

Little Wolf and Bobby dropped the box down by the mound of dirt, all the time keeping their eye on the crows.

"There a couple of shovels in that box, said Buford. "You men start digging."

Buford was standing near the diggers, about to start their dig, when – all of a sudden – a crow, lit at Buford's feet, turned upside down, spread its wings - and began to plead "Please" Please."

"That's no way to beg" said Buford. "You can do better than that."

The crow right side up, bowed its head and began to plead, "Please" "Please."

Buford produced a treat from his shirt pocket and carefully rewarded the bird. "Now can you sing?"

The crow took flight, lit on Buford's shoulder and began to croon, "Damn – Delbert – Damn – Damn Delbert Damn – Damn……

"That's enough," said Buford. "Hello" – "Buford" – "Hello."

"Delbert – Delbert – Delbert," said the crow, taking the treat from Buford's hand. Then it took flight, back into the tree top to a chorus of "Delbert."

The startled young men, after watching the crow's performance, were now frozen to the ground wanting to break wind and run!

"They won't bother you," said Buford. Then a few of the crows in the tree tops took flight west toward the lab.

"You – you- your that ghost of Mucks ain't you?" squalled a terrified Little Wolf, throwing down his shovel.

"Come back here!" ordered Buford. "You got work to do!"

"You – you- your that ghost ain't you!" yelled wide eyed Little Wolf.

"I ain't no ghost – I'm Buford Nitch – Constable of Shadey" said Buford softly. "I told you them birds wouldn't bother you. Now I need you men to dig – right here – and take your time. I'll go get rid of that crowd – now take your time."

Buford, slowly walked back toward the front gate – with flash bulbs going off and reporters calling loudly, "Mister" "Mister!" "Can I ask you some questions?"

"That crow?" yelled a reporter – "Those crows!" – "can you explain them....?"

"Oh they're just some of the local conversational pieces around Shadey," said Buford, smiling.

"Birds don't act like that" said the reporter, gasping for a breath. "Surely there's a reasonable explanation for what we've just seen. How do you explain begging – singing birds?"

"There's just not anything to explain," said Buford, now surrounded by several reporters and photographers.

"But that man" said a reporter, pointing at Harley. "He said – the crows around here are evil spirits. He said – everybody knows it around here – is that what people around here believe?"

"That's Harley's opinion – not mine. Those are just crows – not evil spirits – there're birds – well trained birds – that's all," said Buford.

"Why'd he call them evil spirits?" demanded the reporter.

"I don't know," said Buford. "Now, there ain't no news out here – there's just a hole to be dug – that's all." The he added, "You fellers would be a big help if you'd just go home!"

The reporters were still trying to ask questions – when – several aggressive crows – from somewhere, began an attack, all the time loudly cawing, with an occasional "Hello Delbert" was heard.

"See I told you!" yelled Harley, after getting pecked on the back of his head again, while high tailing it back to the security of his house, all the while dodging crows. "See I told you!"

In the midst of the crow attack – Buford just stood still-unmoving. The men that were standing around were now running for the cover of their cars.

When the crow attack had subsided, Buford was just standing there. – Remembering Molly's advice – "Don't move – don't try to explain animal behavior, people won't believe you."

Several crows seemed to be on guard duty and when anyone tried to get out of their car – an aggressive crow would meet them when they heard Buford.

After a while, Otto started his truck and headed back toward Shadey. Soon he was followed by the reporters.

Buford just stood there watching the last car fade in the distance. Most of the crows now seemed to depart west toward the lab. A couple lit in the tree near the cemetery's east fence – faintly – an audible "hello – hello – hello Delbert – hello."

Now that the crows were gone Buford walked back to the dig site – Little Wolf and Bobby, were now sheltering under the over turned box looking toward the trees.

"They're gone now," said Buford.

"You – you – you're that ghost," said a terrified Little Wolf.

"I ain't no ghost," said Buford. "I done told you. I need you men to dig awhile. I'll keep the crows run off, - and take your time – we don't want no more surprises."

"Harley had said Mucks was buried under that mound of fresh dirt."

"Evil spirits are down there!" yelled Little Wolf.

There on top of the grave site was a number of empty whiskey bottles, all empty – all carefully placed where their neck down.

"What in the hell?" mused Buford, looking at the empty bottles being unearthed and tossed aside.

"Moses, he drown evil spirits Indian way," said Little Wolf.

"I ain't never heard of such stuff," said Buford.

"You no Indian," said Little Wolf. "Indians rid county of evil spirit of Indian way! – Crows evil, too."

Now that the crows were gone, Harley, came out of his house, walked the short distance and was now standing outside the fence watching the dig.

"Harley," said Buford, "What do you know about these bottles?"

"Indian way," said Harley. "Buella wanted evil Mucks spirit drowned. The medicine man make big medicine, the Indian danced Mucks our of spirit world. Now the spirit of Mucks has gone into someone else – maybe you."

"Harley, that's the damnedest thing I've ever heard, said Buford. "How'd you come up with that idea?"

"Indians saw you talking to the crows – and the crows talking to you," said Harley. "The evil crow spirit was in Mucks – now it's in you. You'll see."

<<>><<>><<>>

After about thirty minute of digging, Little Wolf and Bobby excavated the upside down wheel barrow, underneath the wheel barrow was a burlap sack.

"Be careful," said Buford. "Carefully put that sack in the box."

After considerable efforts, with Buford's help, the burlap sack was carefully eased into the box laying on its side, with the sack now pushed into the box, it was up righted and the lid was placed on it.

"Bobby, take that hammer and nails and nail the lid on that box," said Buford. "Let's take this crate and load it in Bobby's truck, we'll come back later and rebury that wheel burrow and bottles. Where's the hammer and nails?"

"Don't know said Bobby – I ain't seen um!"

<<>><<>><<>>

## *Chapter 12 One Friday*

There are Fridays – and then there are Fridays – and then - there was the one Friday – when the one-time constable of the small town of Shadey – became the town's one-time grave robber.

Delbert Mucks – if that was his name – the one-time resident of Shadeys cemetery, was dug up, and on his way, in the back of an old truck, to the little, out of the way town of Reachery – when – once again – for the lack of a better explanation – Muck's evil spirit – or maybe, more correctly – Muck's body re-appeared!

Just outside of Reachery is a sharp s in the highway! Bobby now somewhat "spirit filled" on Buford's "smelling sauce", failed to navigate the s. He ran off the road, flipped up-side-down and skidded to a stop, slinging the cargo, in the back of his truck, box and all, into the creek, knee deep in running water.

Buford skidded to a stop, turned on his flashing lights, bolted out of his car making his way down the ravine, to the accident victims. About the time Buford arrived, Bobby and Little Wolf, somewhat dazed, crawled out of the up-side-down truck slightly scratched up but unhurt.

"What happened?" asked Bobby.

"You ran off the road," said Buford. "You alright?"

Bobby began to pat himself, "everything seems to work," said Bobby, now smiling. "Oh my poor old truck! – My poor truck!"

"Little Wolf – you ok?" asked Buford – looking at the half dazes Indian.

"Me go home," said Little Wolf. "No more dig – evil spirits come back – me go home."

"I'll take you," said Buford, looking for injuries, "I'll take you home as soon as I get done."

"Me done – me walk home," said Little Wolf, now starting to climb out of the ditch.

"Wait a minute," ordered Buford. "I'll take you home – soon as I can – you men go set down in the back of my car until I get there."

Reality was beginning to return. Buford now realized the box was missing. After a diligent search, he spied the box in the creek down below – half submerged in the water.

Buford now waded knee deep in the water, trying to retrieve – the empty box. The lid and the body were missing, Buford now drug the empty box upon the creek bank.

The lid was lodged against the creek bank and a large rock a short way downstream, but the toe sack, was probably submerged somewhere in the creek.

James Dobbs, Reacherys Constable, had been notified by a passerby of the accident just out of town. Now arriving on the scene where Buford's car was parked, lights flashing, with no one around. After examining the wrecked truck, no bodies were inside, nor about. Down below, James saw the crate out of the water, he made his way down the steep slope to the creeks edge. Downstream, James saw Buford waist deep in water, carrying the lid, seemingly searching with his feet, the creek bottom for the toe sack with Muck's remains.

"We got to quiet meeting like this," said James, now waste deep in water. "Who are we looking for?"

"A dead body," said Buford – "Muck's dead body."

"Was he driving the truck?" ask James.

"No" said Buford, "one of them two no accounts, up there in my car, was NOT driving."

"Ain't nobody up there," said James. "They must have took off, they wasn't hurt was they?"

"Not yet," said Buford.

"You think there's a body here in this creek?" asked James.

"Got to be," said Buford. "There's the box and this is the lid – there got to be a body around here someplace."

The two constables continued their search of the creek, feeling around with their feet, at last James hollered, "I found something – feels like a toe sack."

"That's probably Mucks," said Buford, now heading towards James, after placing the box lid on the creek bank next to the box.

Buford now made his way to James – "That ain't much of a sack," said Buford. "We sure don't want what's left of Mucks, out of the sack, floating down the creek."

"I kinda thought folks got buried in coffins, not rotten toe sacks," said James.

"Poor people got poor ways," said Buford. "Nobody around Shadey knowed that old recluse, laying in a floor, dead, for maybe six months, was a somebody. The maggots and rats had him mostly ate anyway. A sack full was about all that was left of him when I got a note stuck in my door, telling me about a body."

"I hate them kind of finds," said James.

The two constables, waste deep in water, began to try to move the sack and its contents toward the creek bank.

"You owe me," said James. "It ain't every day I find myself waste deep in water – knee deep in mud – holding a sack full of a dead man's bones! You owe me!"

"Send the bill to that damned judge," said Buford. "During the last week or so, we learned it about take an act of congress to get a body dug up and moved in Oklahoma. Somehow, this got done in a couple of weeks, explain that to me."

"You mean that credit to the human race, Alvin Thomas?" asked James. "Evidently he's making a name for himself, again."

"I guess he's getting folks straightened out, like he has us in the past," said Buford.

"You know" said James, helping Buford roll the sack into the box. "I kinda wondered about Thomas's interest in Mucks. A few folks around Reachery knew about Mucks, but I didn't know anyone around here knew Mucks was that important."

"Molly and Thomas both did," said Buford.

Mucks and Thomas was classmates back east, eons ago," said Buford. Molly and a Doctor Evens, that came to Shadey looking for Mucks were there at the same time, - so was that damned socialist that got elected president and appointed Thomas a District Judge."

"My word," said James. "The plot thickens now. I didn't know we were so damned important."

"We ain't," said Buford. "They'll be burying us next if we don't get Mucks to Reachery."

The two constables, dripping wet, were now lugging the box uphill to the highway.

"They'll be a big crowd in town tomorrow. Judge Thomas is supposed to make a dedication speech in town at noon tomorrow. The hole's dug, all we need now is a body – I'm really glad I could help find one," said James smiling.

"When I get this body planted again – I'm applying for my pension – I'm planning on forgetting about Mucks, crows, Molly and aspiring judges, making a name for themselves. Maybe I'll write a book about this," said Buford. It'd be a novel, who'd believe this?"

"You write it, I'll read it," said James, smiling. "All we got to do now is get this body to Reachery."

"Maybe it'll fit in the back seat of my car," said Buford. "If that don't work, we'll put it on top."

After considerable effort and grunting – "top it is," said James, smiling. "If you go slow, we might make it another mile or so for the burying."

"Maybe them Indians were right, maybe Mucks is an evil spirit – at least he's getting that way for me," said Buford.

"You ain't superstitious, are you?" asked James.

"Maybe I'm beginning to get that way," said Buford. "You got any crows in Reachery?"

"Now and then, one shows up, why do you ask?" said James, looking at Buford.

"Recent experiences," said Buford. "Just recent experiences – let's get this body buried before the bats – ah – no – crows show up."

<<>><<>><<>>

James led Buford's makeshift hearse, lights flashing, to the Reachery City Park, there were several men standing around awaiting the arrival of the body.

Buford drove up close to the freshly dug hole, with the box on top.

"Where's the hearse?" one of the men asked James laughing at the spectacle.

"It didn't make it. The body is in that box," said James smiling. "We've had to improvise."

Buford and James stood there, muddy and soaking wet as the men took the box off Buford's police car. The men lowered the box into the graves concrete vault, put the lid on the vault, and covered up the grave with dirt. The men set some perimeter concrete forms and poured and finished a concrete slab, all atop the grave – all within two hours after Mucks arrival.

"It's done," said James smiling. "You and Shadey can rest easy now. Surely, no evil spirit can get out of concrete."

At long last, the unbelievable Friday was coming to an end as Buford was able to return to Shadey. Mucks was now in Reachens City Park, enclosed in concrete. Surely peace and quiet would return to the small community of Shadey.

The missing men were seen walking down the railroad, from where they were last seen, it was about a six mile walk to Shadey.

Now alone with his thoughts, in his drive back to Shadey, Buford was now seriously considering turning in his resignation. He had served the citizens of Shadey over twenty years, in one capacity or another. Somehow, digging up dead bodies seemed to Buford beyond the call of a constable's duties. Enough was enough – by Monday morning – maybe he'd compose a letter of resignation.

"Anyone that wants to see me will just have to call the County Sheriff, I'm going home and taking tomorrow off," Buford said to himself. "I haven't had a day off in months."

<<>><<>><<>>

In small close nit communities like Shadey, a lot of what goes on in the world, goes on without making a ripple in Shadey. Every now and then, something upsets the tranquility apple cart.

In the twenty-one years and eighty-seven days Buford had been constable in Shadey, occasionally, a situation would arise. When those situations arose, Buford was able to establish law order and harmony - that usually was the end of that. In time, most issues got lost in the recesses of time.

There were, however, a few stories that would surface that wouldn't go away. The Alvin Thomas issue was one of those things.

The general attitude about Alvin Thomas was universal in Shadey – "Alvin Thomas was no accounts!"

Buford had never heard a good explanation of why he was no account – nor did it matter so long as he stayed away and left Shadey alone.

In the same conversations about Alvin Thomas, usually came the name of old man Grubbs that lived across the river. Whatever their sins were, they were ancient history and unspoken of around Shadey. Thomas and old man Grubbs in conservations were just no accounts.

Most of the information that could be gleamed about Thomas and Grubs came from Harley Fritzs and Jim Bohannan. Both seemed to have an ax to grind about Thomas.

Harley and his wife, the former Buella Sun Song, a full blood Indian, were longtime residents that lived down by the cemetery.

By keeping his ears and eyes open like good law men do, Buford, over several years, was able to piece together most of the conflict between Shadeys citizens and Alvin Thomas.

It had to do with that vast acreage west of Shadey that was owned by that no account boot legger that lived across the river.

Not long after the start of that Vietnam conflict started, all that Grubs property, west of Shadey, for some reason was fenced off and posted, according to Oklahoma's laws, with no trespassing signs and locked gates.

In the eons of past Shadeys history, according to Harley Fritz all that land belonged to the Indians – not a thieving white man. Old man Grubs got Indians drunk on fire water – and then – he stole land for ten cents on the dollar of its real worth.

To add fuel to Harley's fire, several oil and gas wells were drilled on the North end of the Grubs place not long after the old man Grubs died.

For Shadeys Indian community, those hills and forest west of Shadey, supposedly, were sacred hunting grounds. Now those grounds were fence off with smelly gas wells, locked gates and no trespassing signs.

The man that caused all the trouble in Shadeys Indian community was a young Lawyer, from somewhere across the river named Alvin Thomas. Thomas had to be in cahoots with those Grub Worms across the river even if old man Grubs was now dead and buried.

Thomas served notice to Shadeys town fathers that it was Shadeys responsible to enforce the laws of Oklahoma to keep the Indians off private property. The newly elected mayor, Jim Bohannon appealed, the court's order but the order was upheld in district court.

When Buford Nitch was hired by the new administration as Shadeys Constable, shortly after the Thomas victory, both the whites and the Indians were up in arms at Alvin Thomas.

According to the Shadeys grapevine, an Indian by the name of Neva Sun Song owned a sizeable part of that property west of Shadey. Sometime after old man Grubs got possession of the Indian lands west of Shadey Neva Sun Song got drunk, caused a ruckus and was shot and killed over in Reachery along with his boy Reginal. Exactly what transpired in Reachery never came to light in Buford's ears.

The part hard to understand was how Lular, Neva widow, became housekeeper to old man Grubs. Lular and the kids lived in the maids' quarters out back of the Grubs estate.

## *Ch. 13 Demon Possessed*

Buford arose early Sunday morning. As was his usual habit, on Sunday morning, he made his way down to Mona's for his leisurely Sunday morning breakfast.

Out front of Mona's Café was the Gazettes, coin operated news stand.... There for the whole world to see, on the stand's door the headlines:

Shadeys Constable, Demon Possessed!

And there – for the world to see – the photo – a crow standing on Buford's shoulder – cited as proof!

Stunned at what was on the front page of the Gazette, Buford bought his paper, walked into Monas, sat down at his usual table, - bewildered – and began to read the front-page article.

Shortly, Jim Bohannon arrived. He angrily throwed a copy of the State Daily down on the table. The glairing headlines:

Demons Run Rampant in Shadey!

And – there was another picture on the front page – of Buford – with a crow on his shoulder.

"How do you explain these news stories?" demanded the mayor.

"I can't!" exploded Buford. "I can't explain animal behavior! – Nor can I explain damned reporters telling lies – and – I'll tell you something else, I can't explain - who in hell's idea was it to dig up Mucks?"

"You're the investigator," said Jim. "You tell me – it sure as hell wasn't my idea!"

Otto Shorts and Bruce Adams, the Cities Councilmen, now arrived and sat down with the mayor and constable. "I see you've seen the papers," said Otto.

"We've seen um," said Jim. "Now we're all demon possessed – it's all over the front page of half the papers in the state of Oklahoma – Thanks to those reporters – and those pictures!"

"Any damned Indian in the county could have told you white men were demon possessed years ago. Harley's been harping on it for years," said Otto, looking at the mayor. "Those unnamed news sources, those half-witted reporters cited had to be one of our spirit filled neighbors – babbling about Indian superstitions."

"Maybe so," said Jim. "But it don't help none for our constable to be on the front page with a crow standing on his shoulder."

"Well, I didn't plan that," said Buford. "The only half Indian out there was Harley – he was rattling when I got there – Little Wolf – Little Wolf and Bobby got there just before I did - that didn't talk to nobody I know of."

"Harley was out there when I got there," said Otto. "Maybe he's that unnamed source?"

There was a half dozen of note pad pushers and camera bags in my office, not long after Buford went to the cemetery," complained Jim. "Those reporters stormed into my office swearing – they'd been attacked by our demon possessed crows – all the while – Shadeys constable – just stood there like a statue, - untouched – while unsuspecting, honest folks got pecked, swooped at, and ran off – now how's that for a news story?"

"When that army of mad crows showed up, I didn't see no good reason for me to stand around and get pecked," said Otto. "That's when I just got in my truck and left."

"Evidently, so did everybody else!" said Jim. "Those reporters lit in my office, demanding answers and threatening liable lawsuits – like I was out there. Some even suggested it was the city's fault for not protecting its visitors. They said all they came for was to find out about Mucks – not evil spirits and demon possessed crows and constables!"

"I didn't have no idea those crows were going to show up," said Buford.

"Well, that must have been some demonstration you put on down there," huffed Jim. "How long you been talking to crows?"

Since Mucks died, and they started talking to me – like they have you fellows and a good number of Shadeys residents, we all heard them," snarled Buford. "And I'll tell you something else – I ain't demon possessed – despite what Harley or Little Wolf says and people told those reporters, - and I don't believe Mucks was a demon, from hell either! Mucks was just a man like us – that spent his life studying crows."

"Well why didn't those crows attack you like they did everybody else?" demanded Jim.

"I knew to stand still," said Buford defiantly. "I've read Mucks books – it's in there – about crow attacks – so's a lot of other useful stuff about crows – and animal behavior!"

"Well what took you so long to get Mucks to Reachery? The Reachery Mayor called me over here, that afternoon, Friday wanting to know where the body was – and why it wasn't there. He said he had a bunch of men standing around waiting," questioned the mayor.

"I don't believe you'd believe me if I told you," said Buford shaking his head.

"Try me," said the irate mayor.

"Which part you want to hear about – the truck wreck – the missing drunks – the flying box – or about having to fish the body out of a creek?" said Buford, his patients now at an end.

"You're right," said Jim, "I don't believe it."

"I don't believe it either," said Buford. "But it happened."

Bruce had just sat there listening to the arguments and the accusations – "This ain't getting us no place!" piped up Bruce. The body got there and got buried – according to the papers – and Judge Thomas and the Doctor even got to make their dedication speeches. Now I guess every bodies happy – even if those aspiring celebrities wasn't the headlines – we were!"

“Well, I ain’t happy about none of this,” huffed Buford as he stormed out of Mona’s Café. “You’ll be getting my letter of resignation Monday morning!”

After a long period of stunned silence, watching Buford leave – Jim spoke up – “You’re right this ain’t getting us no place.”

A pall set in around Mona’s café – “Where do we go from here?” The mayor asked the councilmen.

## *Chapter 14 One Monday*

Into every man's life, if he lives long enough, it comes time to hang up your badge – if you're a cop.

Buford had been Shadeys Constable nearly twenty-two years. He had given the best years of his life to keeping the order in Shadey – but now, it obviously was time to move on.

After the, unannounced, city affairs meeting down at Mona's, Buford went home, with his collection of newspapers – The Gazette, The State Daily, Sun Daily, and the City Herald. These all carried headlines and photos of Buford at Shadeys Cemetery, citing unnamed sources of Shadeys demon possession and attacking crow population!

Last in the articles about the demon possession was the story of the re-entombment of Delbert Mucks in Reachery. There also was some mention of the memorial dedication in Reachery, by Judge Alvin Thomas and Doctor Robert Evens, longtime associates, and friends of one Dr. Delbert Mucks. Nothing else seemed to be news worthy.

Buford read the articles in each of the newspapers. "How could nearly twenty-two years of service to Shadey come to this?" he asked Kate, his wife of many years, setting beside him.

"That's un called for," she said. "That's not you - you're my husband and the father of our grown children. We know that's not you."

Buford spent Sunday afternoon composed to his letter of resignation.

"I know you hadn't planned on ending your service this way, but we'll survive. Shadey has been our home over twenty years. We have friends here – you have friends here – real friends," said Kate.

"I thought so," said Buford – "up until yesterday. Now I'm not so sure now - I was just doing my job – there wasn't anyone else to dig Mucks up – I still don't know where Moses got off to, after that pow -wow out at the cemetery, he took off some place – Gus said the earth swallowed him, maybe it did."

"I never understood why you had to dig up Mucks in the first place," said Kate.

"That damned Judge Thomas sent the city a court order. We didn't have no choice – the city Buried Mucks – the city had to dig him up – that's all there was to it – it had to be done. How in hell did we know Mucks and Thomas was buddies or that Molly and that kid of hers, wanted him buried in Reachery – like the somebody I guess he really was. For three years, Mucks was just another dead body, nobody claimed. For thirty years everybody around Shadey thought Mucks was some sort of recluse. Now three years later, we find out Mucks owned half the county we live in – had been doing secret research in our back yard and had lots of friends in really high places – all the time the town of Shadey was in the dark – I ain't been doing my job," said Buford. "It's time for me to quit."

"Dear," said Kate. "Your job has been about the law breakers, not law abiders – Mr. Mucks didn't break no laws – either Gods on mans that I know of."

"But half of Shadey is convinced Muck was an evil spirit – and responsible for the multitude of crows and their odd behavior – which, I guess he is," said Buford. "Anyway, from what I saw out at his lab – Mucks was doing a remarkable work – according to Molly and Jimbo, Mucks had to stay away from Shadey and its Indian superstitions – those trained crows just added fuel to Shadeys fire – maybe now – with Mucks gone, maybe Shadey will become quiet again."

Bright and early Monday morning, Buford made it down to his office, the cities secretary gave him his correspondence he had acquired in the last few days. "I saw the papers," Eva said smiling. "You're famous now."

"Not for long," said Buford. "Is the mayor in yet?"

"He came in early," she said. "Mr. Adams and Mr. Shorts are with him – They're expecting you."

The mayors door was open as it usually was, what was unusual was the councilmen were there too.

The three men looked at Buford intently as he entered the mayor's office.

"I might as well get to it," said Buford, handing the mayor his letter of resignation.

The mayor opened the letter, read the brief note – looked at Buford, still standing.

"We – I – I'm asking you to reconsider, your resignation or – at least delay the time of your departure. We – I – the city needs you," said the mayor Jim Bohannon – almost pleading.

"What for?" demanded Buford. "Is there another body that needs dug up some place – I didn't know grave robbing was in my job description?"

"We was in a bind – as you well know." Said Jim. "We couldn't ignore that court order, - nor could we ignore who signed that court order, that jackass is now a district judge."

"Well, I now see myself a liability to Shadey – the community – and to my wife and family. I never expected to see myself on the front page of a newspaper – being accused of being some sort of witch doctor or devil, - for whatever reason – this disaster – somehow should have been averted." Confessed Buford. "I'm just too old for grave digging – it's time for me to go find a new rocking chair."

There was a period of silence and reflection at last Bruce spoke up. "Buford we've been friends and co-workers many years, we're asking you to reconsider – you've served this city very well, for many years – we've had our ups and downs in the past. This is another one of those downs, I'm – we all are – asking you to re-consider."

After another pause Otto said, "Maybe I should have stayed down there with you. Those reporters were asking questions, I had no answers too, - and then – the crows showed up - they swarmed us like a bunch of bees, acting like they were protecting you. I never heard of such a thing. They just didn't seem to be nothing else for me to do, but leave. I wasn't helping nobody."

"I never expected a swarm of crows either," said Buford. "From everything I ever thought I knew, or read about in Mucks book – you can expect the unexpected in animal behavior."

"But you seemed to be prepared," said Otto. "I certainly wasn't – neither was those reporters."

"Alex or Cleo, which ever it was, that lit on my shoulder, I kinda expected," said Buford. "That's why I had a few grains of corn in my pocket. I had a run in with them over at the lab. Alex is a highly trained animal. It took Mucks nine years to train that bird, - according to Molly – an intricate part of that training. The documentation of that training is in Mucks Book. Alex is a highly trained animal – as is Cleo, his offspring. Those animals need protection – not condemnation as some sort of evil spirit."

"We agree, we've read Mucks books too," said Jim, now holding up copies. "We had no idea what we were up against until we got that court order and these books, Buford, we're asking you to reconsider resigning – maybe you could be more help protecting our interest and those animals as Shadeys constable, than you could from a rocking chair."

"How did you come by those books?" asked Buford surprised. "All I've seen was in the college library in Ada – until Molly gave me copies – they are very interesting reading."

"Not long after the mayor of Reachery called, wanting to know where the body was, Effie Mims came storming into my office, - after my scalp again." Said Jim. "She'd been out to see Buella. Somehow, she got wind that Muck was dug up and gone. She was ranting about disturbing the spirit world. She said the Indians had danced Muck out of the spirit world. I didn't even know she was Indian – did you?"

"I heard about the powwow," said Buford. "Big medicine, so I hear."

"Anyway," said Jim, "according to Effie, Now we've unraveled the spirit world – according to Effie – now we got the Indian population up in arms, Effie throwed those books on my desk, stormed out of my office, hollering, "Now see what you've done."

"Good Lord," said Buford, still standing. "Has the whole world gone mad – or is it just us?"

"Oh, there's more," said the mayor. "Judge Thomas has now decided he needs to visit the lab – that's in our county. It's a fact finding tour – along with several Hacks and Reporters running with him. All this is unofficial you understand – hush – hush. He was planning on a big to do by announcing his candidacy for governor at that shindig over in Reachery – Now he's mad at Shadey – again – we've stolen his Thunder."

"If he wanted to tour that lab, why didn't he tug himself across the river like I did?" asked Buford,

"I don't know," said Jim. "The excuse I get is because the Lab is in our county. That lab is on private property – we don't even have keys to the gate – and it's a long walk."

"They ain't no roads to that lab. Surely somebody told him it's a long walk through the bushes." Said Buford.

"Outside of you, none of us has even seen that place, said Jim. Until recently none of us had even heard there was a lab back in that timbers - oh and Mona called, she said some reporter had been snooping around down at her place asking all kinds of questions. Now he out at the cemetery for some reason."

"Maybe I'll go see what he's up to," said Buford.

"Does that mean you'll stay?" asked Jim with a faint smile.

"For the time being," said Buford.

It had been an eternity – three miserable days since last Friday.

Buford left his office and drove the two blocks to Monas Café. As he came in the door he was greeted by several smiling, cheering, locals. "He looks better in the papers that he does in person," piped up someone in the back of Mona's Café.

Buford took his usual seat, Mona brought her coffee urn, "What'll it be?" asked Mona smiling. "I don't get to many celebrities in here>"

"You still ain't got one," said Buford.

"You must be somebody now," said Mona. "There's been a half dozen people in her asking question, - some asking where the talking crows can be found - some wanting to see Mucks grave, - some wanting to see the demon possessed constable. I've had many more strangers in here in the last four days than I've had in here in the last four months – thanks to that story in the newspaper."

"I was wondering," said Buford, "If you seen Bobby or Little Wolf lately?"

"They was in here Saturday night, complaining about wrecking Bobby's truck, and having to walk home. Drunk as usual."

"Was they ok, otherwise?" asked Buford.

"I guess," said Mona. "They was saying something about a big Indian powwow out east of town some place – big medicine – everything is big medicine to them two. Seems the Indians out east blame you, Moses and them for all this trouble of late."

"I guess they're all right," said Buford. "I'll try to run them down after work, they still got work to do."

"They done covered up that hole," they said they was afraid of constables with evil spirits. Every Indian in the county is afraid of the demon possessed Shadey constable now," said Mona smiling. "And all that time I've known you I thought you was just another Demon possessed man."

"I guess that's my new image," said Buford frowning.

<<>><<>><<>>

Out east of Shadey was the reservation – as such. There were several residences and a sizeable building that they called their lodge. The lodge is where they had their get together, there was little – if any – association with the Shadey Community – the -Indian community stayed mostly to themselves, as did the residents of Shadey.

There were a few – a very few folks that had associations with both peoples – evidently both peoples liked it that way – at least that's the way it was.

Harley Fritzs, the half Indian and Bobby Davis were two of them – and then there was Moses – only tolerated by both groups. And there was Effie Mims – the School Superintendent and champion of Indian causes!

Buford made his way down to the Shadey Cemetery. The hole was covered up – the reporter was gone. The whiskey bottles, all neck down, were atop the mound just like they were last Friday, and in the nearby tree were a few crows.

"Well hello there," said Buford.

"Hello Delbert – Hello – Hello – Hello," could be heard.

After a few moments – the crows took wings and flew towards the lab. "That's odd," thought Buford to himself.

Buford went back to his car and drove on North to the river, looking for Little Wolf and Bobby. No fisherman were insight. "That's odd," thought Buford to himself. "Where'd they get off too?"

Buford now made his was out to Moses' shack, - no one was around – he went on down the road to the reservation. As he neared the lodge he was met by a mob of Indians – shaking their fist – and gesturing in a menacing way – "You no welcome, you go home!" They shouted, mouthing numerous obscenities.

Being badly outnumbered, Buford made his way back to Shadey – confused and badly shaken. He had never in all the years he had been constable, he had never before encountered hostility from Indian community!

## *Chapter 15 Ain't Welcome*

In the twenty odd years he had been constable, Buford had never encountered hostility in the nearby Indian Community, nor had his straightforwardness been questioned before – even in Shadey.

It was midafternoon as Buford made his way back to the once secured Shadey, and its friendly people – but ever since the Mucks affair surfaced a couple of weeks ago, one calamity came piled upon another. The last vestige of reason vanished with those headlines, pictures, and articles substantiated by unnamed sources, - and now – there seemed to be an Indian revolt, in the making.

As Buford neared the railroad, he could see Molly and Old Soap making their way to Shadey.

"It's the handsome law man," said Molly with that captivating smile. "How's the world been treating you of late?"

"I'd really like to talk to you about that," said Buford sternly. "Ever since we moved Mr. Mucks, the whole damned world had gone crazy."

A shadow, now cast on that radiant face. "What are you talking about?"

"You know – having to move Mr. Muck's body to Reachery," said Buford staring a hole in Molly.

"What are you talking about – who – moved Delbert's body to Reachery – How did that happen?" asked Molly, standing beside Buford's car, with Old Soap laying down.

"You mean – to tell me – you didn't know about that court order signed by your buddy Alvin Thomas?" said Buford glaring at Molly.

"I know Alvin Thomas – I didn't know he signed a court order to have Delbert's body moved," said Molly now wide eyed.

"Wasn't you and Jimbo at the dedication at Reachery last Saturday?" ask Buford.

"What dedication?" demanded Molly.

"That dedication at that Mucks Memorial over in Reacherys Park. That damned judge and that Dr. Evens, from back east, made big speeches – according to the papers that was quite a crowd over there." Said Buford, annoyed.

"What are you talking about? – Jimbo and I have been out at the lab ever since your visit. We've been working at the lab and staying at the cabin at night. Neither one of us had been off the place - Old Soap and I just came to Shadey to get a few things – you mean Delbert's body has been moved to Reachery?"

"It's been moved – and the whole damned crazy world knows about it – if they can still read a newspaper or watch a T.V. set."

"We don't have any of that junk out at the cabin," said Molly – "you mean Delbert's body has been moved?"

"He's been moved – I had to see to it,' said Buford – we got a signed court order – we didn't have no choice."

"And – Alvin signed the order?" asked Molly, now with tears coming to her eyes. "You mean Delbert's been moved?"

"He's been moved and now the Indians are in an uproar, and I guess you didn't know about that either?" said Buford sarcastically.

"Did he get danced out of the spirit world?" asked Molly, between the tears.

"That's what I hear happened," snarled Buford.

"When did that happen? That's an Indian superstition – Delbert wasn't Indian – why would they do that?" asked Molly confused.

"I don't know why – I just hear they did," said Buford. "A couple of days before we moved Mr. Mucks.

They did it in the middle of the night – during a full moon – it had something to do with - with the crows aggressive behavior and there unusual habits of late – so's I hear."

"And Alvin signed that order?" asked Molly with confusion and denial written all over her once charming face.

"Alvin signed it," said Buford, looking questionly at Molly, then he added, "Maybe we could have appealed that court order?"

"And you say they danced Delbert out of the spirit world," – asked Molly softly, now composed.

"That's what I hear," said Buford, looking at Molly.

"Let's Go!" said Molly to Old Soap, as she turned abruptly and started to walk back down the railroad tracks.

Buford watched Molly and Old Soap walk briskly back down the railroad track.

Buford now, was more unsettled than ever. All his years in law enforcement had not prepared him for this encounter with Molly – in his sole – Buford knew – Molly did not know. He opened the door of his office, slammed the door shut, sat down at his desk and covered his face with his hands, both elbows resting on the desktop, - the nagging question – how could she not know?

A couple of hours later, Buford was about to go home when Molly and Jimbo came into his office obviously upset.

"Mom tells me they moved dad's body to Reachery – I didn't know you could do such a thing!" said Jimbo, loudly! Dead bodies have the right to stay buried – at least they used to."

"I didn't know it either until we got a court order – and a date given," said Buford. "You folks sit down we'll talk about this."

"I don't want to set down – I want to shoot somebody!" said Jimbo, loudly! "The man that ordered it done and the man that did it!"

"I understand your anger and frustration," said Buford calmly. "But we got a signed court order – signed by one Alvin Thomas – District Judge – I take it you know him?"

I've met him – mom know him," said Jimbo. "She doesn't like him – he's a scrowndel!"

"Now with that – I could agree," said Buford. "But we can't disobey a duly signed court order – signed by a district judge."

"Maybe I orta just shoot him," said Jimbo loudly.

"Young man, it's not a good idea to make threats – even if they're justified – we need to talk about this – in a rational manner – I'm sure your mother agrees with me," said Buford calmly.

"I want to shoot him, too," said Molly, wiping her eyes with a tissue.

When Molly and Jimbo had regained their composure Buford asked, "How is it the city of Shadey could get a court order on behalf of the Mucks family and you not know about it? According to James Dobbs some attorney filed that request on behalf of the Mucks family in District Judge Alvin Thomas signed the court order."

"Dad didn't have no family I know of," said Jimbo empathically. "And I sure didn't make no request like that!"

"Well somebody made a request," said Buford. "Judges don't draw a request like that out of a hat – at least they didn't used to."

After a reflective pause Molly spoke up softly, "Son, we should have told you – Delbert had some family…" after another long pause, between the sobs, "He had a …after wiping the tears… he had another son too."

There was another stunned pause for reflection, at last Jimbo demanded, "Mom what are you talking about? – What are you saying?"

When Molly had regained her composure, amid the sobs…"We should have told you….but….it….. it just didn't seem important," said Molly softly…. "He was young once… so was I … once… we were young… at least I was… you came along… we were young back then."

"Mom what are you saying?" demanded Jimbo.

Buford interrupted, "Molly this sounds like something you and your son need to discuss – unless it has something to do with Alvin Thomas."

"It has everything to do with Alvin Thomas," said Molly softly, looking from Jimbo to Buford… "Alvin's sister, Missy….is….is the mother of Daniel Thomas….he's a young lawyer up in Tulsa….supposedly Delbert's other son." At that revelation Molly broke down into uncontrollable convulsions…."I'm so sorry…maybe we should have told you."

"Mom what are you saying?" demanded Jimbo.

"Maybe, we should have told you," said Molly regaining her composure. "Delbert and I loved you dearly, all your life. We've taken care of you, as best as we could as busy parents. That ancient history was never been an issue with me or Delbert. All the other family secrets have been dead issues until Alvin signed that court order – and now – Delbert has been dug up and moved to Reachery.

"What family secret you talking about!" demanded Jimbo.

"Oh there's so much you've never been told," said Molly between the tears. "There's so much you never needed to know – until Alvin signed that court order – and now the Indians will be up in arms."

"What's the Indians got to do with this?" asked Jimbo, wide eyed. "Dad wasn't no Indian, was he?"

"Delbert wasn't an Indian, but his work was always a major concern to them – from the very beginning!" revealed Molly.

"What's bird study got to do with Indians?" asked Jimbo, looking at his mother.

"It has to do with local tribal lore," said Molly. "According to the tribes spiritual beliefs, crows are the mean their ancestor's spirits are carried to the bottom of mother earth. Their eternal happy hunting ground."

"That's preposterous!" said Jimbo. "I don't believe that!

"It's not your belief we're dealing with here," said Molly. "It's what they believe – for many of the local Indians, it's the basis of their existence. It's their religion – and they live by it."

“I never heard of such stuff!” said Jimbo defiantly. “How’d you know about all these Indian superstitions?”

“Son” said Molly, “I was raised here, around the Indians and their superstitions, - in your grandpa’s house. After your grandpa hired a local Indian woman, Lular Sun Song, as his housekeeper and my nanny. Lulars daughter Buella, and I were like sisters growing up, until I went off to college and Buella married Harley Fritzs.”

“Is that them Indians that lives down there in the old shack by the cemetery?” asked Jimbo.

“That’s them,” said Molly. “Buella and I haven’t talked much since she married Harley – Delbert’s work, according to Harley and Buella, is disturbing to the Indians spirit worlds.”

“This is getting more confusing all the time,” said Jimbo, shaking his head. “None of this makes any sense to me. What’s digging up bones – that ain’t Indian – got to do with the Indians spirit world?”

I’ll have to do a little guess work here,” said Molly, now somewhat composed. “Buford said the Indians danced Delbert’s spirit out of the spirit world a few days before Shadey got that court order.”

“What does that mean?” asked Jimbo.

“It’s an Indian ritual – it’s their way of regaining harmony in the spirit world – after Delbert died, a number of crows began to exhibit unusual behaviors – Delbert’s evil spirit was the cause of that behavior, according to the Indian beliefs.

“They believe that?” asked Jimbo.

"That's part of it," said Molly. "When white men caused that grave to be disturbed, by digging up Delbert, that has put the Indian spirit world into turmoil – Delbert's evil spirit has been unleashed. Now the spirit world has to be appeased. The evil spirits have to be eliminated – either crow or man," said, Molly, looking at Buford then at Jimbo. "You're both in grave danger, as is anyone else that had anything to do with disturbing the Indians spirit world."

"I never heard you or dad talk about Indian superstitions as I was growing up, - not even once! I never even heard about such stuff in college!" said Jimbo, wide eyed.

"There's so much you never needed to know growing up," said Molly. "There was me.... there was Delbert... there was my work...there was Delbert's work... and there was you, to love and protect from the world and its evilness. That's all that ever mattered – that's still, all that really matters to me."

"Now that I think about it, I never heard you or dad talk about much of anything as I was growing up – except crows.

All the family I ever heard mention of was grandpa Grubs that lived up there on the hill. There never was anyone else you talked about except dad and his work or your work. Alvin and Missy would come by sometimes – I never knew why."

Alvin's daddy owned a law firm and accounting, and tax service up in Tulsa. George Thomas, had handled several legal affairs for papa over the years. As well as for Delbert, before papa died," said Molly. "Alvin was sent by every six months or so to give me a financial statement. He also – he also," stuttered

Molly, as she began to weep again. "He also wanted money to keep quiet about who Daniel was – child support – or Daniel needed something special – I don't think Delbert knew anything about that. Money has not been much of an issue for me…your grandpa left us well provided for – that property and those gas well are yours - your grandpa and your father saw to that – in spite of Alvin Thomas, on behalf of Buella and Harley Fritzs and their un-substance claim to the property owned by papa."

After listening intently to Molly's confession awhile, Buford interrupted – "Molly, it sounds to me like there may be a law issue at stake here – I have to ask – was Alvin shaking you down?"

He always claimed it was something Daniel needed or child support. It wasn't much - Alvin wouldn't have dared to ask papa or Delbert – I think- no – I know Alvin was afraid of them."

"Mom I still don't understand how Alvin got tangled up in all this," said Jimbo.

"It goes back to our college under graduate days at Outland University, back in our stone age. There was Vietnam protest and happenings – we all were young and wanted to be part of it back them…until we grew up, at least Delbert did. He was working on his doctorate dissertation, I had just met him….I thought Oklahoma might be a good place to do his research – I brought him home to meet papa – as a matter of fact it was an ideal location. Delbert bought that place across the river – the rest is history."

"But I thought you and grandpa owned that place – not dad – obviously – I don't know anything about dad either," said Jimbo.

"We were waiting until you turned twenty-five and maybe settled down to let you know a lot of important things – your grandpa and your dad decided that – not long after you were born – and I've seen to their wishes through the years of your growing up. You'll be twenty-five in a few months."

"Mom what are you saying? I must have grew up in a vacuum," said Jimbo looking at his mother.

"We never told you – it didn't seem important – your daddy was a very wealthy man in his own right, and you and I have always had the means to live comfortable – not – extravagant. Your grandpa saw to that before he died – his assets were put in trust – in mine and your name before he died. Your dad's assets – which are considerable – will be yours when you turn twenty-five. We'll discuss those details – when you turn twenty-five," said Molly, mustering a faint smile.

"I still don't understand. What did Alvin have to do with all this and dads other son?" asked Jimbo.

"Son," said Molly, with a weak smile. "Parents don't tell their children about the sins of their youth, - we never told you – it's not that it wasn't important – none of this conservation was necessary until the ambitious, conniving judge, Alvin Thomas, signed that court order – he wants to be Oklahoma's governor."

"Did you say dad had his own wealth?" asked Jimbo.

"Yes, he had his own wealth, and his own sins, too – before I met him," said Molly. "Delbert was the only child of his aged parents. They both died while he was in school at Outland University. He was seeing a free spirit named Missy Thomas, Alvin's sister, back when they were undergrads."

"I'm getting the picture now," said Jimbo.

"Anyway Missy got pregnant, she said Delbert might be responsible. Delbert didn't argue with her – he just gave her a cash settlement. That was about three years before I met Delbert. By then Delbert's word revolved around crows."

"When I brought him out to Oklahoma to meet papa – they soon made a deal. Alvin Thomas, fresh out of law school, was hired by papa, for some reason, to draw up the purchase contracts for the land and mineral rights of papa's property south of the river. When you came along, there was no questions who was the father of my baby – there never has been – you are papa's only grandchild – the only one he'd ever have."

"Then all this about Alvin Thomas' political aspirations?" asked Jimbo.

"That's what it looks like to me," said Molly. "He's always been ambitious – he tried to get elected student body president at Outland University his senior year. He even tried to run for County Representative, but was defeated by Bruce Adams daddy – he's been mad at Shadeys white population ever sense."

"So that's his anger," mused Buford. "I didn't know that."

"Oh it's deeper than that," said Molly. "Alvin's wife is Harley's sister – or at least she used to be – so is Effie Mims."

Well I'll be damned," said Buford. "Oh, what intricate webs."

"I never dreamed Alvin would do something like this," said Molly, now somewhat composed. "I wonder if Daniel even knows about this. I would have thought he would have better sense."

"When ambition gets in the way of reason, common sense fly's right out the window," said Buford. "Molly I wish I didn't have to tell you – especially not now – but Alvin has sent notice to the city of Shadey that he is coming here on a fact finding mission. He says he needs to visit that lab – someone told him it was in this county."

"There is not anything out at the lab that concerns a damned politician," piped up Jimbo, animated. "It's – a – a – bird sanctuary – on private property – it's privately owned – and funded and by God – he ain't welcome!"

"People in general ain't welcome," said Molly, quietly, "especially him."

"Mom!" demanded Jimbo. "Didn't you just say that place over there belongs to me?"

"When you turn twenty-five," said Molly. "You're not quiet twenty-five yet – I've dreaded that day for years."

"Well until I turn twenty-five, who has the say so in what goes on over there?" asked Jimbo.

"I guess I do," said Molly. "Delbert made me conservator of his estate until you turned twenty-five. Those legal papers are in a safety deposit box, in the bank near our home back east."

"Well if I'm gonna own that place in a few months, don't I have the say so who sets foot on my place?" demanded Jimbo, looking from Molly to Buford. "Ain't a man's home still his castle, or have they changed the laws lately?"

"You have the say so, if your mother says you do," said Buford.

Both men looked at Molly, "well mom" demanded Jimbo.

"I've known all your life this day would come," said Molly with tears coming again. "My baby has grown up and became the man we hoped he'd be," after a long pause, Molly smiled, - "it's your place."

"If that's my place, then judge or no judge, Alvin Thomas ain't welcome on my place," said Jimbo, emphatically. "That's all there is to it – When's that scoundrel supposed to be here? I'll tell him myself!"

"Wednesday at 10," said Buford. "Maybe I can head him off before he gets here."

"Don't bother," said Jimbo. I'll be glad to tell him myself."

"Maybe I should be the one to tell him," said Molly. "Maybe he'll listen to reason."

## *Chapter 16: One Tuesday: Uprising*

It was well into the evening when Molly and Jimbo left Buford's office. As unsettling as the lengthy conversation had been to Buford, how much more it must have been to Molly and Jimbo.

Buford just wanted to go home, but the mayors' door was open. That always meant an open invitation for another talk with the mayor about city business – Otto and Bruce were there also.

"Looks like you've been busy," said the mayor as Buford came in. "I see you've had important guest – they looked upset when they left here."

"They were upset," said Buford. "I would be too is someone had laid on me what Molly laid on that young man a while ago. He's had to get old in a hurry. For starters, Molly just told him he owns that place over there. Jimbo says he's gonna run Alvin's ass off his place – Molly says she'll try to talk to him – and Alvin too."

"This sounds like Wednesday might be an interesting day," said Jim.

"But I thought Mucks son wanted Mucks moved to Reachery," piped up Otto.

"Not that son," said Buford. "It seems Mucks may have another son, according to Molly."

"What in the world!" exclaimed Otto. "How many more kids did Mucks have we don't know about?"

"Just one more boy is all I've heard about," said Buford. Here's the part you'll really like – the other son is Alvin's nephew – he's that young lawyer we've been hearing about making waves up in Tulsa. He's the son that partitioned the court, and Uncle Alvin signed it."

"Good Lord," said Jim. "Do you believe that story?"

"I don't have any reason not to believe it," avowed Buford. "Jimbo and Molly swear they were out at the lab while all this was going on. They say they didn't know about that court order to move Mucks' body, nor about that dedication ceremony over in Reachery. According to Molly, digging up Mucks is going to cause and Indian uprising."

"What Indian uprising – I haven't heard about Indians on the war path unless that's what Effie Mims was threatening," said Jim.

"According to Molly," said Buford. "Digging up Muck, has turned the Indian spirit world upside down – and here's another gem or information you fellows will relish. Effie Mims is Harley Fritzs sister – so is Alvin's wife, Mary, if they are still married."

"Oh my God," said Jim, perplexed. "Friend, you're not the only one around here that don't know nothing about nothing. What else is there we don't know about?"

"Well," said Buford, "the Indians are madder than we are – us digging up Mucks has brought the local Indian spirit world to a screeching halt. Unless the spirits are appeased, they ain't no way for the good crows to carry the spirits of their dead to the happy hunting ground."

"You mean we got an Indian uprising on our hands too?" said Otto, concerned. "I heard there was a big powwow going on out at their lodge."

"All I know for sure about that is that they told me to get lost," said Buford. "I was out there looking for Bobby Davis and Little Wolf earlier today. For the first time they said I wasn't welcome."

"You've been busy, ain't you?" said Bruce in his quiet manor.

"I just hope this day is over with," said Buford. "I just want to go home."

"Me too," said the mayor. "But I'm afraid the earth may open up and swallow me."

"That's about how my world has gone for the last three days," said Buford. "I'm going home – maybe tomorrow, the sun will start shining again."

"I hope you're right," said Jim.

<<>><<>><<>>

It was about three am when Buford was awakened by his phone:

"Buffe, this is James – I got Molly and Jimbo here in my office – somebody set fire to that house of theirs down on the river, and probably torched the lab too! They've also destroyed that cable tram."

Buford was now wide awake. “Do they know who done it?”

“Molly thinks it might be Indians,” said James. “No way of knowing for sure – at this un Godly hour. I been out for a look see, but not on your side of the river. We’ll be in Shadey sometime after sun up.”

“Are they all right?” asked Buford.

“They’re a little rattled, otherwise they seemed to be ok,” said James. “They were up at the big house, when the fire started – it seems Old Soap set up a howl. When they got down there, there wasn’t anything left except smoke and ashes. They said it looked like the lab was torched too – the trams been trashed too.”

“Ask Molly if there’s anything I can do until you all get here?” said Buford, over the phone.

After a long pause, James said, “Molly said you could shoot Alvin.”

“I’d be tempted,” said Buford.

James arrived at Buford’s office a little after eight. Jim, Otto, and Bruce were in Buford’s office.

“James,” said Buford to the new arrival. “This is Jim Bohannon, Shadeys Mayor, this is Otto Shorts, and there is Bruce Adams, our Councilmen.”

“Glad to meet you,” said James, shaking their hands. “Jimbo and Molly will meet us down at the retreat, they said the gate would be open.”

“You know where to go,” asked Buford.

"This ain't my turf," said James, smiling. "I'll let you lead me around by the nose."

"Ok let the show began." Said Buford, heading toward the door. "You fellers are welcome to come along – it's a long walk."

"I'll go," said Jim.

"Me too," said Bruce. "Maybe Molly will need me for something."

"You're hoping," said Otto, smiling. "I'm too old, I'll just stay here and run the city until the mayor gets back."

Buford lead the way past the cemetery, down the path that lead to the retreat. When they arrived, the retreat was in ashes, with whiffs or smoke evident. Jimbo car was parked, but no one was around.

"The labs about half mile down that trail," said Buford. "I guess they're on foot."

The men began their walk down the trail down the path toward the lab. There just didn't seem to be much to talk about, as they made their way to the lab.

When the men arrived, Molly and Jimbo were groping among the ashes.

"Delbert's lifetime of work – up in flames." said Molly, with tears. "For what reason?"

"I can't answer that," said Buford. "Sometimes we get caught in an evil web, for some unknown reason, - maybe this is one of those times."

Molly looked intently at Buford, "That sounds like something Delbert would have said."

"Molly is there anything I can do?" asked Buford, looking intently at Molly.

"Not now," said Molly, brushing the tears. "There don't seem to be no pieces left to pick up. Why all this? – A lifetime of Delbert's work, up on smoke. Have you noticed – the crows are gone too. This was their home and life's work too – why them?"

Jimbo came to his mother's side and embraced her. "Mom lets go. There nothing we can do here now. – let's go home."

"When we know something, I'll call you," said James. "We've still got lots of work to do."

"I know you do – well all do," said Molly, amidst the tears with her son embracing her. "Delbert's life time of work – Now up in smoke – for what reason? For some fools political ambition? For out and out ignorance? Why? You men find a reasonable answer that I can understand!"

"Mom, we can't do no good here, let's go home," said Jimbo, then he added, - "I'll be over in Shadey at ten in the morning – in case Alvin shows up!"

"Find an answer I can understand," said Molly softly, as Jimbo led his mother back sown the trail.

"We'll try," said Buford.

We'd all like some answers," said Bruce. "Maybe Molly just pointed out what we are up against – there's no cure for evil – it just runs its course."

"You probably right," said Jim, watching Molly and Jimbo vanish into the trees.

The men began to take note of their surroundings. "We got work to do," said Buford. "James, let's go walk down to the tram – maybe there's something?"

"There not much left around here for Alvin to look at now," said Jim. "From what I can see, this must have been some kind of place."

"It was," confirmed James. "I was over here three or four times over the last twenty years – Molly was always my guide – usely, Delbert was up in the tree tops, when we got here."

"When I got my Molly tour, it was Jimbo up there," said Buford, pointing up the scorched tree those men were now standing under.

"You suppose all the grief came because of that damned court order?" asked Bruce.

"Oh, I don't know," said Buford. "Maybe it's deeper than that."

"Maybe it is," said Bruce. "Muck was around for maybe thirty years – I never knew much more than his name…"

"Let's walk down to the trams landing," said Buford to James, after walking through the rubble and taking more pictures.

"It's a fair walk," said James to Jim and Bruce, standing nearby.

"We'll poke around here awhile," said Jim. "We're not used to those long walks, we'll see what we can find."

The two law men made their way down the path to the trams landing.

"It looks like they hacked at that support cable, unwheeled the cage and cut the pull rope," said James, as they walked down the path. "That's about all I could make out with a flashlight this morning."

When the men got to the landing, the trams cage was faintly visible about a hundred yards downstream, near the river's rock bluff.

"I wonder if we can fish it out," said Buford. "Maybe we can salvage enough of the pull rope to snag it with, before it washes on down the river. It might still be useful if they decide to use it again. This tram and that railroad bridge is the only ways to cross the river – otherwise, it is a forty mile drive."

"We can give it a try, if we don't fall in – Molly said her and Old Soap liked their strolls, walking crossties to Shadey. She said Old Soap wasn't welcome at the lab," said James.

The law men fought their way through the dense vegetation and briars on the river bank getting as near as they could to the tram's cage that was mostly submerged in the water.

"You still a cowboy?" asked James. "Maybe you can snag that little doggie like you used to."

"I don't get much practice anymore," said Buford smiling. "I gave up calf roping for the law – right now – I don't know why."

After several attempts Buford lassoed the cage, and both men began to drag the cage to the rivers six foot high bluff.

"Iron's heavy," said James. "I wonder why it didn't sink in the quick sand they say is around here."

"Don't know," said Buford, tugging on the rope. "I guess I flunked quick sand classes, back when we were in rooky school – Lord – that's been thirty years."

"Time flies while you're having fun – it drags while cage tugging," said James, between the grunts.

After considerable efforts the two men were able to drag the cage up to the steep river bank. "Now what?" asked James, panting like a lizard.

"Let's tie this thing off so's it won't wash away, and get us some help," said Buford, wheezing.

After a brief visual examination of their catch, "That looks like something's still in it, - that could almost be a body," said James, getting down on his hands and knees for a closer look – "I believe it is!"

"I believe you're right," said Buford, now laying flat with his head over the bluff. "Let's get this thing out of the water."

"Whoever that is must have been trying to get rid of the evidence, when that cage was crow bared off the cable – he would have to been standing on the cage's edge to get at that pulley."

"If that's who done it – he must of fell in the cage and drowned when it fell into the river," said James. "Or maybe somebody put him there."

"That's how it looks to me," said Buford. "Maybe the four of us can lift this cage – and the body out of the river – I'll call Jim and Bruce, maybe they can hear me."

"You who!" "You who!" yelled Buford. "Bruce! Jim! We need help!"

After a few moments, listening for a reply, Buford hollered again, "Hello!" – "Hello!" – "You Hoo!" – "We – need help!"

"We're coming," came a reply, barely audible, from a distance.

Soon from across the river came a faint "Hello – Hello – Delbert – Hello."

"Well I'll be damned," said Buford, smiling. "Did you hear that – there's still some crows around."

"I hope it was crows," said James, smiling. "I've been hearing lots of ghost stories lately. I've even been reading there in the newspapers lately."

"Me too," said Buford, looking across the river – "Mucks ghost stories."

Buford stood there, eyes fixed, looking toward the sound coming from across the river – he hollered – "Hello – Hello-Buford – Hello."

Soon two crows made their way to where Buford was standing – landed at his feet – flopped upside down and began to plead, "Please!" "Please!" "Please!"

"You can do better than that," said Buford, retrieving some grains of corn from his shirt pocket, "Now beg."

The crow's right sided themselves and began to beg, "Please!" "Please!"

"Ok – that's enough – now can you sing?"

Both crows lit on a snag nearby – eyeing James now a statue.

"They're bashful today," said Buford. "Alex – if that's you can you sing?"

The crow cocked its head – this way – then that – it began to groan. "Damn Buford damn – damn Buford damn – damn…."

"That's enough," said Buford, smiling. "Alex took his grains of corn from Buford's hand. Both crows took flight back across the river.

Soon there was a chorus of "Hello – Delbert – hello," heard from across the river with an occasional, "Buford" and "Molly" uttered.

James stood there wide eyed. "I got a whole new appreciation of how law men spend their time in Shadey – no wonder you made the news."

"Ever since Molly gave me a tour of the lab, I've been popular with the crows," said Buford, smiling. "They've got me into the habit of carrying corn around in my pocket."

"Uh huh," said James, smiling. "That sounds reasonable to me."

Soon Bruce and Jim arrived to help. "Was that Muck's ghost we heard talking?" ask Jim.

"Nah," said James grinning. "It was just Dr. Do What talking to the crows."

"I'm not sure if it was Alex or Cleo," said Buford, with a slight smile. "I was sure glad to see them – and I'm damned glad there wasn't no reporters or cameras around this time."

"Me too," said Jim. "That one picture, the other day, has caused at least two thousand words of speculation and innuendos' around the state, the last week or so."

"What is that thing?" asked Bruce, peering at the mostly submerged cage.

"It's a trolley cage," said James. "They road in that thing, suspended on a cable across the river. It looks like that might be a body in all that river trash."

With considerable effort, the four men were able to man handle the cage and its contents up the bluff to dry land.

The four men, after their strenuous ordeal, were standing around the cage, appraising their catch of the day on the rivers bank.

"Let's see who we got her," said Buford, removing the rivers accumulation of trash after taking pictures.

"Well it ain't no Indian," said James, looking at the body.

"He said he was," said Buford. "He's one of our locals."

"How do you suppose he wound up in the river," asked Bruce.

"I aim to find out, said Buford. "The Indians around her will know – in the meantime, I got to get the county corner out here – maybe he can tell us something about that gash on his head."

"I take it you know this bode?" asked James.

"We all know this man," said Buford. "Somebody's got a lot of explaining to do."

# The Ghost of Delbert Mucks

# Part 3

## *Chapter 17 Not Again*

It had been a very long day – it wasn't even noon yet!

James Dobbs was on his way back to Reachery - he had work to do. Jim Bohannan had the town of Shadey to run, after he called the corner. Bruce Adams, the councilman, had a store to run, Constable Buford Nitch had errands to run, and the spirit of Harley Fritzs – the dead Indian body – was on its way somewhere.

Harley Fritzs claimed he was an Indian. According to Shadeys Indian population, Indians, alive or dead, were Indian problems!

The only Indian around Shadey that had any dealings with dead bodies, white or Indian, was Moses – he'd been out of pocket several days – and then there was Harleys Indian wife Buella, she had to be notified.

Buford made his way east out of Shadey towards the old shack where Moses lived.

"Is Moses around?" asked Buford.

"Him gone," said Snowbird. "Him bad medicine – Skywolf say so!"

"Uh huh," said Buford. "You know where I could find him?"

"Him bad medicine, him go cross river," said Snowbird, pointing north. "Him bad medicine, him stay gone – me shoot him."

"Uh huh," said Buford. "But do you know where I can find him?"

"Him gone longtime, no come back, me shoot him," said Snowbird.

After the informative conversation with Snowbird, Buford got in his car and headed east toward the reservation. The last time he was out there, yesterday, looking for Bobby Davis and Little Wolf, he was met with hostility. For over twenty years, he'd always been met cordially and with respect, until yesterday. Something had changed – he didn't know what to expect today.

The tribe's headquarters was next to the lodge. Several men were standing around out front of the headquarters and lodge entrance.

Cautiously Buford stepped out of his car and approached the men with all eyes fixed on the constable. "I need to see Chief Big Buck, or Sly Wolf – official business."

One of the Indians entered the lodge. In a few minutes, Sly Wolf came back out with him.

"What you want?" asked Sly Wolf, sharply eyeing Buford.

"I got a body out by the river – Harley Fritzs," said Buford.

"Him no Indian," said Sly Wolf. "Him just wanna be!"

"Well Buella's Indian. She needs to be told," said Buford.

"She know," said Sly Wolf, "Him drown in river."

"Uh huh," said Buford. "Then you know who set them fires out there too?" said Buford, looking intently at Sky Wolf, the Indians Medicine Man.

"White men, with evil spirit, set fires," said Sly Wolf, as he turned around and walked back into the lodge.

"You no welcome," said one of the young men, standing around now shaking his fist – you evil spirit."

"I'm no evil spirit!" said Buford, loudly. "I'm Buford Nitch – Shadeys Constable."

"You evil spirit! You make crows evil too!" said the young Indian.

"Those crows are just black birds – they're not some sort of carrier pigeon for spirits. Those crows are big black birds that have been taught to talk and do tricks – that's all!" said Buford, defiantly.

"You evil bad medicine – so's crows" said the Indian, now going into the lodge.

<<>><<>><<>>

It was now midafternoon. Whether the knot in his stomach was hunger or something else, he was on his way, after leaving the lodge, to Mona's Café. It was way past time for breakfast.

"What'll it be?" asked Mona, pouring his coffee. "I hear you got up early this morning."

"Breakfast – my usual if I can get it this late," said Buford, mustering a smile, looking at Mona. "Just in the sake of interest, how is it you can hear so much cooped up in this place all day?"

"I keep my ears and eyes open," said Mona smiling, "besides Otto was in here early this morning alone."

"Oh, I've tried that open ears and eyes stuff," said Buford, with a faint smile. "Lately all I get is bad news or something about evil spirits or Muck's ghost, and I ain't any evil spirit – I'm just a man trying to do a day's work for a day's pay – that's all"

“We always though so,” said Mona, looking at Buford, “I guess you’ve heard there’s a big pow wow, taking place out on the reservation – its big medicine, so I hear.”

“I’ve heard that,” said Buford, “but I haven’t heard why – by chance have you?”

The evil spirits got to be appeased,” said Mona, looking at Buford. “It’s Indian stuff – digging up Muck’s body, for whatever reason, after they had danced him out of their spirit world has toppled the local tribe’s world off its axis.”

“I never heard of such stuff,” said Buford, hanging on to Mona’s words. “How’d you hear about this stuff?”

“Evidently those Indians heard about or read about that crow attack out at the cemetery last Friday where everyone got pecked, except you,” said Mona.

“I just stood still,” said Buford. “I read about that in Muck’s book -that’s all – that wasn’t my idea.”

“It’s what them Indians believe – that’s the problem – reason ain’t got nothing to do with any of this – you know that as well as I do – it’s their superstition.” Confided Mona in a whisper. “Bobby Davis and Little Wolf are scared to death – so is Moses – they are laying low – so’s I hear. It seems they are too close to the white people. The tribe’s mad at them. By chance, you didn’t happen to hear where I could find them – have you?” asked Buford, in a whisper.

“Not exactly,” said Mona, softly. “Moses has kin, maybe an uncle – so’s I hear somewhere over across the river – he’s kin to them Sun Songs over around Reachery.”

"Sun Songs you say? Buella's kin to them folks too," said Buford, barely audible. "You suppose they're kin?"

"Huh?" asked Mona. "What'd you say?"

"Oh, I was just thinking out loud," said Buford, smiling. "Sometimes you're sweeter than an angel maybe I'll kiss you someday."

"That angel stuff would be bad for my reputation – don't go spreading that around," said Mona, dead panic. "Kate might get wind of it. You're going to have trouble enough hanging onto your scalp as it is, so's I hear."

"How's so?" asked Buford.

"Harley was in here yesterday afternoon, all worked up, rattling about the disturbance of the spirit world – saying he had a solution – I never thought much about it," said Mona. "He's always got a solution to everything; you know how he is."

"I know how he was," said Buford, quietly. "We fished him out of the river this morning,"

"You mean Harleys the one that set those fires to get rid of the evil crows, then drowned himself to appease the spirit world?" said Mona. Quietly, they she added; "I don't think Harley planed on drowning himself – that just wasn't Harley."

"You're just full of surprises today," said Buford. "How'd you get wind of something like that?"

"I just listen to the wind blow and put two and two together," said Mona. "Bobby and Little Wolf staggered in here, drunk as skunks about closing time, yesterday, bragging about moving on to the white world. This was their last supper as

Indian, they said. They said they had resigned from the tribe and were retiring up north some place. They said we'd see um no more, - I told um I wouldn't miss um."

"You know," said Buford, taking Mona's hand. "Maybe you are an angel after all, and you would have made one hell of a big city detective. Thanks for whispers floating upon the wind." Now he kissed Monas hand. "Thanks for the info."

"That done it – I'm telling Kate," said Mona in unbelief.

"She won't believe you," said Buford, smiling.

"Probably not," said Mona shaking her head, retrieving her hand. "I don't believe it either. Kate says the only thing your passionate about anymore, is your work."

"Uh huh," said Buford. "What else did you and Kate talk about?"

"I ain't telling you," said Mona, smiling. "Oh and be careful. Kate needs you in one piece!"

After eating breakfast in the middle of the afternoon, it was way past time to check in with Eva, Shadeys shared town secretary.

"The mayor and the corner are in your office – they just got here, from out yonder. I hear it's been a long day already for everybody," said Eva, smiling.

"Very long," said Buford, "and it ain't no where over yet."

The mayor and Mitchel Rends, the County Corner, were setting talking, when Buford came in. "You know anything new?" asked Jim.

"Lots of stuff I don't like," "Am I missing anything new around here?" asked Buford.

"Oh yeah," said Jim. "When I got Mitch out there – the body was gone!"

"Dead bodies don't just jump up and take off!" Said a stunned Buford. "Dead bodies used to stay where you found them, until recently, around here!"

"Well, that one didn't stay put," said Jim. "The cage was still there but the body was gone. It looked to us like the body got back in the river – ain't that right Mitch?"

"That's what it looks like," said Mitch. "He probably had some help getting back in the river, I hope. That must have been a quiet place out there before the fire bugs showed up, I'd never heard of a place like that around here, before."

"We hadn't either," said Buford, "until we needed a solution to the crow problem – then came that court order to unearth the man that built that place – now we got an Indian uprising on our hands, and a ghost in top of every tree, according to the Indians. All that, thanks to that judge that orders bodies dug up that wants to be governor."

"Everybody knows he's a credit to the human race, - at least anybody that's had a run in with him know that," said Mitch, smiling.

"That's just part of our troubles," said Buford, dealing with reality. "Dead bodies don't jump up and run off, at least they didn't used to! Somebody knows a lot more than they're telling – I aim to find out why," Sky Wolf said, "Harley drown, and that

Buella already knew it before we did. When I asked him about them fires out there, he said white man evil spirits set them."

"How'd he know all that?" asked Jim, shaking his head in unbelief.

"He didn't say – he just said him drown and Buella knew, and walked away. I guess their shindig was about to start – every Indian in the county seemed to be out there – all dressed up in paint and feathers – and nobody out there would talk to me."

"Well, the cities had its own problems today, too," said Jim. "While we were out poking around at the lab this morning, Effie Mims came in my office and climbed all over Otto, ranting about evil spirits and dead bodies. She said she wanted her brother's body out of the river, and she said it was our job to get it for the burying. Otto said he thought she'd flipped out of her gourd or something. How was Otto supposed to know that body we drug out of the river this morning, was Effie's brother? Explain that to me!"

"Like I said," said Buford. "Somebody knows a lot more than they're telling. Somebody know who the body snatcher is – and I aim to find out!"

"Well, when you find out, I'd sure as hell like to know who steals dead bodies," said Jim, animated.

"You men's mystery is just getting deeper," said Mitch. "If or when you find a real body, I'll be glad to examine it for you – if it's dead – maybe he'll show up."

"He was dead! We all saw him!" said Jim, almost apologizing. "He was laying crumpled up in the floor of that tram's cage when we left to call you."

"Maybe that body was another one of them ghosts you folks got haunting around Shadey," said Mitch, smiling and standing up to leave,

"Friend, thanks for coming on such short notice," said Buford. "Maybe our dead body will show back up before too long,"

"Next time – if you need me – call." Said Mitch, winking at Eva. "I thought maybe you'd talk to me over a late lunch over at Mona's – I'm so hungry – if they find their phantom body give me a call."

"You can bet on it," said Eva, smiling. "We seemed to be overrun with evil spirits and ghost lately."

So's I hear," said Mitch, smiling. "I've been reading the papers lately. Buffee ain't never looked so good as he did in the papers last Sunday."

"You can't believe all you read in the papers these days – even about Shadey and it constable," said Eva, staring at Mitch, grinning.

"Oh, I don't," said Mitch. "Up around Ada, we got our own ghost stories – but Shadeys ghost makes a lot better reading."

"I didn't know you could read," said Eva, smiling.

"I just looked at the pictures," said Mitch. "Buffee's got a tough act to follow. I hope his newfound fame don't go to his head and get him scalped, see you around - now I'm going to have to deal with Mona all by myself – maybe she's forgot me? Call me sometime."

"Nobody ever forgot you – even if they won't to – anyway. I'll call if we have need of a weird wolf," said Eva, smiling. "Oh, tell sis hi! I'll drop-in next time I'm up your way – you're buying – I'm having steak."

## *Chapter 18 Now What?*

Michael Rends, the Counties Corner, had just left for Mona's. The mayor and Buford were chattering trying to make some since out for the day's events when the phone rang.

"Buffee, this is James. "I got a couple of young Indian men over here you might be interested in – I found them up a tree, in the woods not far from that burned out cabin. They ain't talking to me but they act scared to death. They said they'd talk to you."

"You found, two Indians up a tree? Sounds reasonable to me, the way things have been going lately," said Buford, smiling.

"It's all in a days' work anymore," said James. "Old Soap tree'd them; evidently Soap don't like Indians, - you orta seen them birds setting on a limb up a tree," snickered James. "Me and Molly was heading towards the lab when Old Soap broke loose from Molly and headed down the river. When we got there, them dudes was up a tree, like tree'd squirrels. They stayed there, up a tree, until we got there, and Molly called Old Soap off. Molly says you know them.

"Uh huh," said Buford. "They got names?"

"Mostly they been babbling about evil spirits and about that dude drowning. They say that dude fell in the river when somebody crowbarred that trams pulley off the cable. Evidently, they saw us drag that tram's cage out of the river, from across the river, - they might have been in that tree hiding, when Soap found them."

"That's about what we figured had happened," said Buford. "Too bad I missed the show – did you find anything else of interest? You say Molly was going to the lab?"

"Yep," said James. "Jimbo was over there already – according to Molly, about a couple hundred yards upstream from the tram. You can wade the river when the rivers down, how's bout you – you solved any mysteries lately?"

"Nope – now that you asked – I got a new one," said Buford. "That body – we pulled out of the river this morning – would you believe – it has up and vanished – it took off before Jim and the corner got out there – how's about them apples?"

"Uh huh," said James, after a pause, "sounds about right – you won't me to come help you find it – like last time – you still owe me!"

"I'll be over your way shortly," said Buford. I'm gonna see if I can find Jimbo and see if there's anything around that tram's cage – oh – that Sun Song clan over there, I need to run them down while I'm over there – can you give me directions?"

"I'll go with you," said James. "You're gonna stir up a hornet's nest – we ain't gonna be welcome – I'll tell you about it when you get here. They don't like law men visitors."

"Nobody likes seeing us coming. I'll be there as quick as I can," said Buford, hanging up the phone.

Jim was still standing there, "I heard enough to know you're onto something. Anything I can do to help?"

"I hope so," said Buford. "Don't wait up – I'll call when I get back- oh, and would you call Kate and tell her I'll be late for supper – again."

"Maybe I orta go to Reachery and let you go talk to your wife," said Jim, smiling. "She hates hearing from me – you're going to get me flogged."

"Better you than me," said Buford, smiling. "Be back when I get back."

<<>><<>><<>>

After James's phone call, it was obvious things were not settling down - as a matter of fact, Buford was barraged with more unanswered questions – who snatched the body?

Maybe he had missed something out at the lab that morning. Buford decided to make another long walk to see if Jimbo could shed some light on the mystery.

Buford started down the county road resolved to find Jimbo out at the lab. As he neared the cemetery, several cars were present and a number of people he recognized were congregated in a circle.

A chill ran up Buford's spine as he stepped out of his car and started toward the congregation. Someone recognized Buford – instantly all eyes turned to face him.

"You're not welcome," yelled Effie Mims, raising her voice and shaking her fist. "This is a private funeral."

A number of the young men began to advance toward Buford.

"You men BACK OFF!" yelled Buford, unstrapping his service piece.

"You not welcome," yelled Little Wolf – one of the hostiles. "You evil spirit!"

"You men stand back!" ordered Buford, Loudly, "Before I unloose hell's fire on you! Now stand back!"

The men stopped their advance, glaring a whole in Buford with his hand on his service piece.

After a few moments decision making, Buford ordered, "Little Wolf – you come over here!"

Buford could see the terror in the young Indian's eyes – he made the few steps toward Buford slowly.

"Little Wolf, you know me," said Buford, with his hand on his service piece. "You know, I mean what I say – if I don't get some straight answers, I'm going to bring the wrath of God down on your young ass – you understand me!"

"You evil spirit!" said the terrified young man. "You that evil crow ghost!"

"Little wolf – you pay attention to me! I'm not an evil spirit – I'm Buford Nitch, Shadeys constable – But I'll be the devil himself if you mess with me – do you understand me?"

"You that ghost spirit." Said Little Wolf, wide eyed.

"No I'm not – yet!" said Buford, directly. "Who died?"

"You evil spirit!" said the terrified young man.

"Young man – I'm going to run your young ass into Shadeys jail in a heartbeat – you'll be there until hell freezes over – now I won't to know – now – who died?"

"Him – Him – Harley – Him drown," said Little Wolf, pointing toward the freshly dug grave.

"How do you know that – and how did Harley get here?" demanded Buford, staring a hole in the young man.

"Him drown.... bad spirit...you....evil....sp...," said Little Wolf, as he crumpled upon the ground.

"Now see what you've done!" screamed Effie Mims, as she rushed toward Buford and the prostrate young man. "You've KILLED HIM!"

"He ain't dead," said Buford. "I've seen him pull this trick before – to much firewater."

"He's dead!" yelled Effie Mims.

"No, he ain't," said Buford, as Little Wolf began to moan. "Evil...now you – Miss Mims lets me and you have a little talk-either here – or in my office- that body – how'd it get here?"

"You go to hell!" yelled Effie defiantly. "Indians and their evil spirits killed my brother – now they're going to pay! – I'll see to that!"

Effie was now cradling Little Wolf in her arms – "he sick."

"He's drunk," said Buford, now turning his attention to Bobby,

"Bobby – come over here," said Buford, sternly.

Bobby standing with his hands in his pockets with his head down, began to slowly walk toward Buford.

"Bobby, what do you know about this?" Demanded Buford, softly, staring at the young man.

"Nothing," said Bobby, looking at the young man.

"Bobby – talk to me, "said Buford. "How'd that body get here?"

"Him drown," said Bobby.

"Uh huh," said Buford. "That ain't what I ask you. How'd Harley get here?"

"He fell in the river," said Bobby.

Bobby began to cry still looking at his feet with his hands in his pocket.

"Harley Drown," said Bobby, softly.

"Bobby that ain't what I asked you – how'd Harley get here?"

After a long silence, - we – we found him, said Bobby.

"Un huh," said Buford. "Where did you find him?"

"By river," said Bobby, still sobbing.

"Now Bobby," said Buford, - "How'd Harley get by the river?"

"Don't Know," said Bobby. "Him by river – down by old bridge – honest – him by river by bridge – him drown – ask Little World – we just go fishing."

"Uh huh," said Buford, "Little Wolf."

"Him by river – him drown – you evil spirit," said Little Wolf, now setting, cradled by Effie Mims.

"We didn't need your help anyway!" sneered Effie. "You satisfied now?"

"Not quiet," said Buford. "We'll talk about this later – get on with your burying – we'll talk about this later."

<<>><<>><<>>

It was well into the afternoon when Buford got to Reachery, after the confrontation at the cemetery. Molly, Jimbo, and Old Soap were there waiting, in James's office.

"I hear Old Soap has been applying himself of late," said Buford, patting Old Soap, now standing up.

"He has," said Molly. "Soap set up a howl this morning – that's how we knew there was something wrong – looking south, we could see that glow - I don't know if Soap smelled something. When me and Jimbo got down there, everything was on fire. The real loss was that lab – that was Delbert's life's work."

"I feel for you," said Buford. "I'm sorry, but I have to ask you some questions – do you have any idea who did this and why?"

"Maybe," said Molly, brushing away some tears. "The who was probably Harley and maybe – those two young Indian men Old Soap tree'd. The why – that's grounds for speculation. Why, problem goes back to the thirties and early forties – before I was born."

"Then you think this is a lot more than just recent occurrences," asked Buford.

"A lot more," said Molly. "It goes back to my papa buying all that land from the Indians. I've never known all the details for sure, that sale took place long before I was born. What I do know – there has always been hard feelings for years between papa and those Indians out on the reservation."

"I've heard there's been some bad blood between some of our Indians and your Indians," offered James.

"You mean all those Indians don't get along?" asked Buford.

"Not hardly," said Molly. "Neva Sun Song authorized the sale of all that land, on your side of the river, to papa. Back then, Neva had substantial authority with the tribe. After the sale, Neva fell into disfavor with some of the tribe. I guess they drummed him out of the tribe. Sometime later, Neva got control of several thousand acres of land on this side of the river. After my mama died, papa hired Lular Sun Song as his house keeper and my nanny."

"That sounds unusual," said Buford.

"It was," said Molly. "Lular lived in the maid's quarters, out back with all those kids of hers and Nevas. There was always a lot of Indians around as I was growing up. The younger kid's usually stayed out back of papa's house with Lular and the older kids stayed with Neva. Quite often they'd be some sort of ruckus, papa would have to referee, - especially when they got to drinking."

"Is that how the brawl came about we've heard about?' asked Buford.

"Indians get along about like white men do when they're drinking," said Molly. "Anyway, when Big Buck and Sly Wolf were young men, they were some kin to Neva. There was a drunken brawl over at George Thomas's place, outside of

Reachery, it was a – a – you know, one of those places. When the brawl was over, Neva and Stink were dead and Moses was half dead. Not long afterwards, Neva's widow moved into our house, along with Buella. I never knew any of the details of how all that came about. Papa sent me back east to Outland U. Maybe James can spread some light on that Brawl."

"Not really," said James. "All that was way before my time here in Reachery. It's been quite some time, but I've read that report filed by the Reachery Constable, back then – a Monroe Fritzs. No charges were ever filed –lack of evidence."

"You mean there was two killings and no charges," said Buford.

"The jest, I got, it was an Indian thing – you know how those things go." After a few moments of quiet – James muttered – "Fritzs – Fritzs –hum – you supposed that Monroe Fritzs and that Fritzs we fished out of the river this morning was some kin?"

"Harley was Monroe boy," said Molly. "Harley and George's boy Alvin were running buddies back then. Eventually Alvin married one of Harley's sisters –Mary. Both of those young men were at that ruckus when those killings took place."

"Some of this is beginning to make since," said Buford. "There's a lot of people, with a lot of axes to grind around here, and there's a whole lot some folks won't keep quiet about."

"Growing up around a house full of Indians that was don't talk much, most of what I got was hear-say, and not much interest to me back then. I had lots of other interests.

"I've heard Jim and Otto mention that you were an object of considerable interest back then," said Buford, smiling.

"I was young back then," said Molly, showing embarrassment smiling. "Mostly, I think the Indians on the reservation though white men – my papa – and latter Delbert, stole the Indians land – especially when they discovered oil and gas on Delbert's place. Harley's been harping on that for years. Every now and then, some court challenge would arise – it has a couple of times in the past."

"I see," said Buford. "But is that why the Indians are so hostile of late?"

"When Delbert bought that place over there, he fenced, and posted it, mostly to keep his work isolated. Some of the Indians maintained the land was their sacred hunting grounds. That lawsuit went nowhere. Later – somehow – Harley – not long after papa died, brought suit on behalf of Buella, Harley's wife, alleging she was papas' daughter and was entitled to half of papas' assets. There was no proof just accusations."

"Then is the motive revenge?" asked James.

"That's possible," said Molly. "Alvin Thomas, fresh out of law school, litigated that suit on behalf of Harley – Delbert hired a real lawyer that made them look like the fools they really are – at least that is how I see it – now Alvin's a District Judge."

"Is there more to this?" asked Buford.

"Them Thomas's have been up north of Reachery for eons," said Molly. "If I had to guess, Alvin didn't know what would happen when he ordered Delbert exhumed – at Harley's insistence, but then again, I'm guessing. Alvin probably did not know the Indians had danced Delbert out of the spirit world, a few days earlier."

"Is Buff's picture in the paper what set the Indian off?" asked James.

"It certainly opens old festering wounds," said Molly. "For thirty years, according to the Indians on their reservation, Delbert's research was troubling to the spirit world."

"I see," said Buford. "This thing between Delbert, Alvin, and Harley is tangled up with that ruckus again – is that it?"

"It has certainly opened up old wounds," said Molly, now composed. "Delbert and I were able to keep Jimbo out of all this after papa died."

"Well, I'm not out of it now!" said Jimbo, having listened to this latest conversation.

"Son let me deal with Alvin this one last time," pleaded Molly. "James has told us that body they pulled out of the river was Harleys and Buford said the Fritzs woman, Mary, Effee, and Buella were burying Harley in the Shadey Cemetery a while ago. My guess the Indians will want his body back in the river to appease the spirit world – it's an Indian superstition – I don't know if Harley died accidently or if the Indians planed it – I just know – with Harley dead – the spirits can be appeased if they can somehow get Harley's spirit drowned."

"Good Lord," said Buford, shaking his head. "You don't suppose?"

I'd almost bet on it," said Molly. "Those spirits have to be satisfied – one way or another – you may be in danger too – if the Indians believe you're the spirit of Delbert now."

It was late in the afternoon, near sundown when James and Buford made their way toward the Sun Song place.

"Old Ernest Sun Song runs that place. Them Sun Songs got four or five sections of land down on the river, I guess all those Indians on that place are related. If you have a run-in with one of them Sun Songs – one way or another you got to deal with Ernest – He fancies himself as chief or witch doctor or something anyway, if it's one of them Indians, you have to deal with Ernest, one way or the other."

"That about how it works on my side of the river," said Buford. "Is that Sun Song place a reservation over here?"

"I guess that's what it is?" said James, on the drive toward the Sun Song place. "I just know there's a passel of them Indians out there. I've never heard of these Indians having anything to do with your tribe. When something comes up – I got to know what bunch of Indians I'm dealing with. As you know, the Indians on my side of the river and the Indians on your side are different tribes – with different agencies."

"That is kind of a hassle sometime," said Buford. "But unless I'm mistaken – those Sun Songs used to belong on my side of the river."

"That's about how I see it," said James. "That's their lodge and office or whatever it is up ahead, who you after anyway?"

"Moses – they tell me he may be the real one you've heard about," said Buford, smiling.

"Is he the one in the Bible or the one Molly said got shot over here – right after the flood," asked James, grinning.

"He probably the one Molly said got shot over here when them two dudes got killed – back in the stone age - he's got kin on my side of the river. Them two young bucks you got in jail and Harley's wife are Sun Songs, too."

"Uh huh," said James. "While you was out and about, I ran down to the abstract company up in the county seat – that Neva Sun Song, bought that place over here not long after old man Grubs bought half the counties on your side of the river – this Earnest is Neva's boy. I ran down a couple of Reacherys old, old timers – that heard about the ruckus – they said old Ernest was there too. How about them apples?"

"I'm beginning to think half the population of the state was at that ruckus," mused Buford. "That's five names we got that was there – four are alive and mad and one is dead."

The two constables continued the conversation on their way to the Sun Song place. Buford spoke up, "Moses, if he's here, and if he's sober – he can probably shed some light on all this Indian uprising. Moses is one of my missing Indians – for some strange reason he has been out of pocket for a couple of weeks – he's the one I got to be a grave robber – Moses is a Sun Song so's I hear. He's some kin to Harley's wife; Harleys that body we drug out of the river, that somehow got from where we left him to Shadeys Cemetery half a day later, How's about that?"

"You think this Moses can unravel that mystery?" asked James, parking in front of the lodge.

"Maybe," said Buford. "The two young half Indians, I lost over here last week, swear they found old Harley, out of the river, not far from where we left him. If they're telling the truth – then two young bucks, you got in jail, are Moses and Snowbirds sons. I've had run-ins with them in the past, - there's usually three of them."

"This orta be interesting," said James, getting out of the car. "We ain't gonna be welcome – I never am."

James and Buford entered the tribe office next to the lodge. – "I need to see Ernest – official business," said James. "This is Buford Nitch, Shadeys Constable."

"The young man stood up, looked intently at Buford, "You evil spirit – you not welcome."

"We didn't come here to discuss spirits – we came to see Ernest," said James.

"Ernest in city – pow wow," said the man.

"Uh huh." Said James. "You in charge around here, then?"

"What you want?" ask the young man.

"We need to see Moses – if he's around," said James. "Two of his boys are in my jail – you suppose you could find him?"

"Him drunk – someplace," said the young man, "him sleeping."

"Maybe you can wake him," said James. "We'd like to talk to him."

"Go home," said the young man – "I find him – I wake him – I tell him – go home."

"We'll be in my office – for a while," said James, - "in case he happens to wake up."

James and Buford now on their way back to Reachery while discussing business.

"James?" asked Buford, "This Ernest – what kind of powwow do you suppose he's at?"

"I was wondering the same thing," said James. "The paper said Thomas was making a to-do up in the city – you suppose Ernest knows something Thomas wants to know? Like maybe – something about a fire at a lab across the river?"

"It does make one wonder, don't it?" said Buford. "What are the odds Alvin will be a no show over in Shadey about ten tomorrow morning?"

"Me think me smell a rat," said James, smiling.

It had been a very long day. James and Buford stopped at the local café for a bite of supper.

"Well, well, well," said Buford, after looking around his new surroundings. "Up jumped the devil – there's my long-lost Indian."

"Is that your Moses?" asked James. "I've been seeing him around for the last week or two."

"That's him – let's go talk to him," said Buford, leading the way to where Moses was setting alone.

"What you been up to lately?" asked Buford, setting down. "This is James Dobbs – an old friend of mine. He's Reacherys' Constable – you know him?"

"Me see – no know," said Moses.

I's out you place, looking for you," said Buford, looking at the old Indian. "Snowbird said you'd took off – you's bad medicine. Now I hear the Indians don't like you."

"Mad woman," said Moses. "No want man anymore – me leave."

"Uh huh," said Buford. "Anything you want to talk about?"

"Bad woman," said Moses. "Mad at me, cause Sly Wolf mad at me."

"Moses," said Buford, looking intently at the old Indian. "I kinda hate to ask – but – what do you know about Harley?"

"Him drown," said Moses. "Him fall in river."

"How'd you know that?" asked Buford.

Sly Wolf tell Snowbird. Snowbird tell boys. Boys tell me."

"Uh huh," said Buford, looking at Moses. "How'd they do that? Two of them is in jail now."

"Why they in jail?" asked Moses, now wide eyed.

"James caught Joe and Shoo up a tree out by the river – he's Reachery Lawman," said Buford, pointing at James. "He's out investigating a big fire."

"Them drunk?" asked Moses, now looking at James.

"Didn't seem to be," said James. "More scared than anything else. Why you suppose they was out there?"

"Buella wants Harley home – send Joe and Shoo after him," said Moses. Snowbird send Mew after me. Now Snowbird mad – want to shoot me – cause Sly Wolf mad."

"Uh huh," said Buford. "That fire out there – you set it? – Maybe your boys helped?"

"Harley not set fire. Him in river. Buella sent Joe and Shoo."

"I see," said Buford. "How'd Harley get back in the river after we pulled him out?"

"Joe and Shoo see Harley in river," said Moses, "Not on bank."

"Moses," said Buford, looking intently at the old Indian. "There was three fires set and a tram tore up – that's a lot of doing for one old man like Harvey – don't you thank?"

"Maybe him have help – my boys," said Moses. "Buella send Joe and Shoo – want Harley home."

"You have any idea who could have helped Harley?" asked Buford.

"Indians – not Harley," said Moses. "My boys no set fire – Buella send them after Harley."

<<>><<>><<>>

The two lawmen were in James's office comparing notes when James's phone rang:

"Yep, he's here," said James, handing the phone to Buford.

"Buffe," said Jim, "I got a call a while ago – seeing old Alvin Thomas decided not to come for a look see out at Mucks lab tomorrow - seems something personal came up."

"Do tell," said Buford. "Me and James figured he'd be a no-show. My guess, somebody told him about a fire down here – that somebody probably told him he wouldn't be welcome down here either."

"Sounds like you're on to something," said Jim.

"I'll tell you all about it when I get back to Shadey – it'll wait until I get back," said Buford. "Oh, was my wife mad when you called her?'

"Maybe you'd better throw your hat in the door first, when you get home," said Jim. "Kate made mention of something about an anniversary – seems she had plans!"

"Oh Lord," said Buford. "She's been in the planning mood for a week or two – thirty-five years she's put up with me. Have you any idea how much grief this is going to cost me in the long run – if I miss supper."

"Maybe you better come home now – before she locks the door," said Jim.

<<>><<>><<>>

## *Chapter 19 Wednesday*

Buford arose early Wednesday morning and headed to his constable's office in Shadey. Jim Bohannan, the mayor, was in his office next to Buford's, the mayor's door was open - that was an open invitation for an early morning consultation, the councilmen, Otto Shorts, and Bruce Adams were all there, also.

"Good morning," said Buford, all smiles. "You men are up early this morning."

"I see you're still alive," said Jim, smiling. "Was Kate mad when you finally got home?"

"I just sweet talked her," said Buford, grinning.

"You better done better than that," pipped up Otto. "That'd never work with Rachel."

"Well, I hope it's as good of a morning for Shadey as it is for you," said Jim. "Maybe the sky will quit falling."

"It can't be all bad if that jackass, Alvin Thomas decides to stay under his rock," said Buford. "Maybe we can have a little peace and quiet for a while.

"You said on the phone last night, Alvin probably knew about that fire out at the lab. How do you suppose he found out about it that fast," asked Jim.

"A little guess work and a lucky break goes a long way sometimes," said Buford. "When James and I went out to the Sun Song's place haunting Moses. It seems Ernest Sun Song had just left for a powwow up in the city where his old buddy Alvin

Thomas just happened to be. A little later we ran across Moses over in Reachery yesterday.

"Is that where he'd been?" asked Otto. "We could have used him the last few days if he'd been around."

"I guess so," said Buford. "He got crossways with Snowbird – again – I guess she ran him off – again. Them Sun Songs over in Reachery are his kin folks – So's I hear – seems brother Ernest puts up with Moses when Snowbird runs him off."

"I didn't know he was a Sun Songs," said Jim, surprised. "I've seen him around Shadey for years, but I never dreamed he was a Sun Song, I just thought he belonged to that bunch of Indians over at that reservation east of here."

"Well Moses is a Sun Song – so's Buella, Harley's wife, I guess you knew that – didn't you?" asked Buford.

"I knowed he'd be around some when I's trying to court Molly," said Otto. "They was always a passel of them Indians over around old man Grubbs house and around Reachery – back when I was young – they all looked the same to me back then- except Molly never looked like no Indian!"

"I never heard of them Sun Songs until recently," complained Jim. "Now I guess we're gonna be overrun with them."

"They're going to get a lot of my attention," said Buford. "When I got to Reachery yesterday afternoon, James had two young men in jail. He caught them down by the river, that old dog of Molly's had um tree'd. Them two young bucks was Joe and Shoo. Thems the two youngest boys of Moses's.

"Did them young men help Harley set them fires?" asked Jim.

"Me and James don't think so," said Buford, after talking to Moses a while, I got a feeling there was a lot Moses didn't know. Him or Mew probably told Ernest there was a fire and he knew Harley had drowned.

"Do you believe Moses?" Jim asked.

"Maybe – probably," said Buford. "I've known Moses for a lot of years. Even if he is the towns drunk, I've never heard him speak with a forked tongue. I can't say that about some of them other Indians we have to deal with like Big Buck – especially like Sly Wolf."

After a pause, Bruce asked, "them two young buck – do you know why they were out there?"

"According to Moses," confided Buford, "Buella Fritz sent them two young bucks, her nephews that hang around a lot around the Fritzs house, after Harley, before he got into much trouble. She wanted him back home. Moses said them boys of his got there in time to see Harley and the cage in the water. But supposedly everything was fine when they got there. The boys was supposed to go back home, Snowbird sent Mew after Moses."

"That's quite a tale," said Otto.

"It's reasonable," said Buford. "When James got um," he said, "they was scared to death. Babbling about evil spirits and about Harley being in the river, and they couldn't help him."

"Then was they somebody else out there helping Harley set them fires?" asked Otto.

"Maybe," said Buford. "I don't know if Harley set them fires or not – at least not now. Anyway, somebody must have seen us drag that cage and body out of the river – and somebody – probably a superstitious Indian shoved Harley's body back in the river to appease the evil spirits."

"Do you know who set then fires," asked Bruce – and that gash on Harley's head – you got any idea how that got there, but how'd he get back out?" asked Otto.

Our real stroke of luck was that Bobby Davis and Little Wolf decided to go fishing, and found old Harley washed up on that trash around that old bridge Butress.

"Well I'm damned glad old Harley got out of the river," said Jim, off handed. "Maybe that'll keep Effee Mims off our ass for a while – unless Otto wants to deal with her again."

"It'll be fine with me if you or Buford deals with that woman next time she gets mad about something," said Otto, grinning.

"We'll let Bruce do it," said Buford, softly winking at Otto.

"No we won't!" said Bruce loudly. "I've had her in my store – more than once – mad!"

"Oh well," said Buford, now back to business. "There's still a dead fly in our ointment. How's Sly Wolf on our side of the river and Earnest Sun Song on the other side – mortal enemies – know about Harley drowning several hours before we did?"

"Seeing how its Indians we're dealing with, they was probably sending smoke signals, burning down the lab," said Otto, smiling, then added; "I'll tell you one thing, I'm glad old Harley got out – after hearing Effee squall about her brother being in the river – either dead or alive, I'm glad he got out!"

After a few moments of diversion, Bruce asked – "This Earnest Sun Song – what's he got to do with all this?"

"Earnest is the oldest of Neva's Sun Song's off springs. He's also Buella Fritzs brother. Moses is one of that bunch of Neva's kids too – so was Reginal – he's that Stink- we've heard about."

"You mean Moses and Buella are brother and sister?" asked a stunned Jim. "I'd never of guessed that. I've seen Harley and Moses together a time or two over the years."

"Blood thicker than water, or at least it used to be," said Buford. "But when blood is the basis of a feud – all gets to be fair in love and war."

"Is this Indian uprising we're hearing about a blood feud?" asked Bruce. "This Neva – why's he so important – I ain't never heard of him either."

"Maybe a little pertinent, ancient history, is needed here," said Buford. "Neva was a Mucked Muck in the tribe over here, years ago. He's the one that arranged the sale of all that land to old man Grubbs, - evidentially that didn't go down well with the tribe. Anyway, over at George Thomas, place, a beer dive outside of Reachen, there was a brawl – about that sale – Neva and Stink got killed and Moses nearly was."

"That's that ruckus I heard about when I was trying to court Molly," said Otto. "That's about the time she took off – it was years before I saw her again. When she come back, she had that school age kid with her."

"Uh huh," said Buford. "As I was saying, George Thomas and Old man Grubbs was in Kahoots of some kind. That George Thomas is the daddy of our pain in our butts, Alvin Thomas."

"Well now," said Otto, "that's interesting."

"You'll probably be real interested in who else was at that ruckus," said Buford, sorta smiling. "Earnest Sun Song, Harley Fritz, Alvin Thomas, Sly Wolf, and Big Buck – all were young men back then. Of some interest, to you fellers, - the Reachery Constable back then, that investigated that ruckus was one Monroe Fritzs – Harley's daddy – no charges were ever filed – lack of evidence – how' about that?"

"My word!" said Jim, animated. "Is that what we're dealing with, now?"

"That's a start," said Bufford. "Digging up old Delbert Mucks – when we did – after our Indians had danced Delbert out of their spirit world – opened up a festering wound of hostility between Chief Big Buck and Medicine Man Sly Wolf on one side and Ernest Sun Song, Alvin Thomas, and Moses on the other side, with Harley Fritzs, Effie Mims and Mary Thomas – then maybe half Indians stirring the pot of discontent. And then – there's the crows! Their periocular behavior of late, thanks to Delbert and his work – for thirty years – now there's absolutely no room for reason and pagan superstitions in the same world we live in."

I always thought all those Indians got along," said Jim.

"You'd a thought so," said Otto. "Seems to me like they did. Of course, Indians don't talk much to white people. And old Delbert and his doings really caught us by surprise too – didn't it?"

"Not much caught me by surprise until recently," confessed Buford. "But I didn't have to do much digging until I knew better – especially if you got superstitions, ignorance, and political ambitions the driving forces."

"I agree," said Bruce, after a pause. "That is a lot to contend with all at one time – that damned court order upset the apple cart, didn't it?"

"What was there about digging up old Mucks that set all these wheels in motion that got all these Indians, on both sides of the river, in an uproar?" asked the mayor.

"If you remember?" said Buford. "It wasn't until we buried Mucks that we started getting all those complaints about the crows, and their unusual behaviors and attacks.

Old Harley's encounter was the first we heard about it, but then, Effee Mims one of Harley's sisters, filed that complaint – demanding action."

"I got to admit," said Otto. "That was some unexpected behavior we was seeing and hearing about in our crow population – especially down on the river and later out there by the cemetery."

"Until I read Muck's books, I couldn't make sense, at all, out of that strange crow behavior we was seeing around Shadey," said Buford, empathically. "I was almost beginning to believe in those ghosts they said was around here."

"Me too," said Jim. "I guess those Indians east of here, still believe the ghost of Delbert Mucks is still around here some place – at least that's what I hear around town – those pictures in the paper last Sunday didn't help none."

"You bet they didn't," said Buford, apologizing. "I really regret those pictures in the papers, and the section, from unnamed sources, that the town of Shadey was demon possessed."

"Well," said Otto, "it sure made Shadey and out town folks look bad."

"Well, as sure as there is a hell – I didn't plan that crow attack, - and I can't explain animal behavior. I just did what Molly had told me, and what I had read in Muck's books – if the crows attack, stand still. That was spelled out in Mucks books, that Molly helped write – so's a lot of other good advice, about crows and people."

"Buford," said Jim, concerned. "There's a bunch of folks - especially our Indian brothers around here that are convinced you're that new – evil spirit – of Delbert Mucks."

"I ain't no evil spirit!" yelled Buford. I'm just a man – that's all!"

After Buford's outburst there was an uneasy quiet in the mayor's office.

After a few minutes of needed reflection, Bruce spoke up softly, "Friend – we know – you're no evil spirit – quite the contrary – but – we're dealing with a substantial number of misguided, ignorant and superstitious folks – that don't. You know that as well as we do – if not better. When reason departs – no matter why – ignorance, stupidity, superstitions and insanity rear its ugly face. This little town of ours – that we're responsible for – is now having to deal – face to face – with that ugly face."

There was another period of quiet in the mayor's office:

"I'm – I'm," – said Buford, softly. "My outburst – I'm so – so ....."

"No apologies allowed around here," said Jim, cutting Buford short. "We got a town to take care of. – It's a full-time job lately, we got those damned ambitious politicians causing havoc – we got an Indian uprising brewing – and – we got = we got – who knows what coming next!"

"That, next maybe here now," said Otto, looking out the window. "Looks like twenty or thirty Indians in paint and feather, are heading toward out little city."

"Maybe we better call the County Sherriff," said the mayor, with concern in his voice, after looking out the window. "I'll have Eva call the Sherriff – she can tell him we got a situation on our hands over here – we may need help!"

<<>><<>><<>>

Looking out east from the third story window of James office, in the city hall, Otto had spied a mob approaching town.

The mayor, the two council men, and Shadeys constable stood at the window looking east at the mob making its' way toward town, still a good way off.

"It's the whole damned tribe," exclaimed Jim. "That's Big Buck and Sly Wolf leading that mob – what do you suppose they're up to?"

"I guess I better go see what they're doing," said Buford, now turning around, heading out the door down the hall to the elevator, as Jim's phone began to ring.

"Bruce, see if you can catch Buford before he gets away. James is on the phone," said Jim

Soon Buford came back through the door, "What up?"

"There was an ashen look on Jims face as he handed the phone to Buford.

"They're what?" asked Buford, loudly. "Where they at now....? "... uh huh, ... thanks."

"I gotta go," said Buford, rushing out the door.

"What in hell has happened now?" Otto demanded, wide eyed.

"That was James," said Jim. "That bunch of renegades, from across the river, armed to the teeth, are headed to the cemetery – they may already be there – Ernest Sun Song, Moses, and a half dozen men are going to Buella's house to make sure nobody disturbs Harley's grave – according to James Dobbs, they may be down there now."

"How did James know?" ask Jim.

“Maybe I can be some help to Buford,” said Bruce, heading out the door.

“We’ll all go!” said the mayor loudly – “Otto – you mind the store – Eva – call the county sheriff – tell him we got a situation here – we may need help.”

I’ll call,” said Eva.

“Otto,” ordered Jim, “Call James Dobbs over in Reachery – get some details if you can – tell the sheriff what we’re up against.”

<<>><<>><<>>

When Buford, Jim, and Bruce got to the cemetery – several armed men could be seen setting on Harley’s and Buella front porch. Several cars were parked around - one was a limousine.

“You don’t suppose –“sputtered Jim – “that jackass – surely he’s not here!”

“Harley and Buella is family, so’s Effee, that’s her car over there,” said Buford, pointing to the car by the limousine.

“Looks like the gangs all here,” said the mayor, obviously annoyed – “happy days again.”

Buford turned the flashing lights on his car and parked it across the driveway – “I’ll go see if anybody will talk to me,” said Buford.

“Be careful,” said Jim. “We got your back.”

As Buford approached the house several men stood up – “Moses – what’s this all about?”

“Me visit sister,” said Moses. “You know me brother?”

“We’ve not met,” said Buford, extending his hand.

The old Indian squinted his beady eyes – not offering his hands. "You that evil spirit, you not welcome."

Buford stuck his thumbs in his belt, stood there looking at the ground – slowly, lifted his chin – and stared at the old Indian – "This is not a social call," said Buford, "and I didn't come down here to discuss evil spirits – back yonder, a ways," said Buford, pointing toward Reachery, "is twenty to thirty men headed this way. I'm going to head them off - if I can – we don't want a blood bath down here. Visit with your family – stay on the porch – I'm not asking you – I'm telling you – Stay on the porch! We'll handle this!"

"You that evil spirit people talk about," said the old Indian Ernest, now wide eyed.

"Not as evil as I will be if you get off this porch," said Buford, staring a hole in the old Indian. "I mean what I say!"

Buford slowly turned around and slowly walked back down the path to his car.

The men, and now some women stood there, all eyes fixed on Buford as he sat down on the front bumper of his car, as if he was unconcerned. Occasionally looking toward Reachery. Soon Jim and Bruce got out of Buford's car with shot guns and sat down on the bumper beside Buford, - waiting!

Otto had called James Dobbs in Reachery and had talked to the county sheriff. The sheriff and six deputies would be on their way soon, a forty-minute drive. The mob now on main street of Reachery, were in a circle around Big Buck and Sly

Wolf – in full view of a number of Shadeys citizens, including Otto looking out the window.

"The phone rang," it was Eva.

"Mr. Shorts, there's a Molly Grubs out here and a gentleman," said Eva. "Ms. Grubs says Buford is expecting them, ..."

Before Eva could finish talking Otto was out of Jim's office, grinning from ear to ear.

"Molly is that you – is that really you – as beautiful as ever," said Otto, extending his hand. "It's been a long time."

"You're still blind as a bat," said Molly, smiling. "Maybe thirty years?"

"Got to be – and this young man must be Jimbo – Molly and I go back a ways," said Otto, shaking Jimbo's hand vigorously. "It was your mother's charm and beauty that blinded me back then," said Otto – "She went off to college and I went off to war, - it's so nice to see you again – what can I do for you- Bueff's occupied – at the moment," said Otto.

"We're here to meet Alvin Thomas – he's not going to be welcome on Jimbo's place – there's no lab to see now."

"I'm sorry about the fire," said Otto. "But we've heard that jackass – uh – judge- is not coming -at least that's what we've heard – maybe Buford can shed some light on that."

"I wonder why Alvin changed his mind – I – we was looking forward to running him off," said Molly. "Will Buford be back soon?"

"We got a – a – a situation brewing," said Otto. "Buford – Buford – he's occupied."

"I'll bet he is," said Molly. "That tribe – all decked out – that will soon be heading to the cemetery. That's probably got his interest. Is that where he's at? – Is he down there alone?"

"Jim and Bruce are down there with him – the sheriff and six deputies will be on their way soon – I got to meet 'um," said Otto.

"Let's go," said Molly to Jimbo. "Maybe we can be some help."

"Molly," pleaded Otto. "Please stay out of this – at least be careful – look out for your mother," as Molly and Jimbo headed toward the elevator.

"What a woman!" said Otto, shaking his head – "what a woman!"

"So I here," said Eva, smiling.

Molly and Jimbo eased their way past the congregated Indian mob and headed south, down the road. As they neared the cemetery, they could see Buford's patrol car with lights flashing and three men setting on the bumper.

Jimbo pulled up next to the patrol car.

"Well now," said Molly, smiling. "I never expected to see Shadeys handsome law men, setting on a bumper out here on a lovely day like this."

"Molly," said Buford. "Why you out here?"

"Jimbo and I are just out taking in the sights," said Molly, smiling, getting out of the car. "Maybe you handsome men could use some company – oh I see Buella has company – oh, and I guess more is on the way!"

After Molly got out of the car, Jimbo moved his car out of the road and parked in front of the cemetery. He got out, opened the trunk and brought out two automatic weapons that he laid on the hood of Buford's car.

"Mom said we were going hunting after Alvin left," said Jimbo. "Is it all right if we stay a while and visit?"

"Molly why you here?" asked Buford. "Alvin ain't coming."

"Oh he's here. That's his car," said Molly, smiling. "He's developed some degree of passion for his kin in his old age. Now he's got family ties – I'm sure he'll be glad to see – uh – old friends."

"Molly, why you here?" asked Buford.

I'm just making a social call," said Molly. "That's all – son lets go make a call on those – uh – nice people."

"Ok mom," said Jimbo, smiling. "Is all right if I leave the guns – they're loaded, and the safeties are off."

"Molly why you here?" asked Buford again, looking from the guns to Jimbo to Molly.

"Oh, those other guest will arrive in about thirty minutes," said Molly. "Our howdy – do's will be over by then – ta, ta," said Molly, walking up the lane toward the house alongside Jimbo.

"What in Hell is she up to?" ask Jim, shaking his head.

"I don't think I want to know," said Buford, watching Molly walking toward the house.

As Molly approached all the men stood up, giving space. She kind of nodded at the old man as she and Jimbo entered the door of Buella house.

About twenty minutes later Molly and Jimbo came out of the house, she spoke to old Ernest and Moses a few minutes, casually, Molly and Jimbo walked back toward Buford, standing there in disbelief and stunned silence as were Jim and Bruce.

Molly and Jimbo made the few remaining steps. Jimbo retrieved the two automatic weapons engaged the safety and put them back in the trunk of his car.

"Molly! Why....?" Asked Buford.

"Oh, handsome law man, could you move your car a few feet – Alvin and his wife Mary – especially Mary – has decided they have urgent business to attend to up in the city – they'll be leaving shortly," said Molly, smiling.

"Molly," asked Buford, softly needing something to say. "I guess I've asked you before, why you here?"

"I just needed to pay my respects to old acquaintance," said Molly, softly. "Would you move your car? Alvin has decided to go to the city."

Soon a man and a well-dressed woman got in the limousine and came down the drive as Buford moved his car. The Mayor Jim Bohannon and the Councilman Bruce Adams just stood there, with their shot guns trying to blend into the near scenery.

When the limousine left, going toward Shadey it was soon surrounded by a number of noisy Indians yelling loudly and shaking their fist. Slowly the car threaded its way through the mass of demonstrating Indians.

With the commotion on the road several Indians, including old Ernest Sun Song and his brother Moses began to meander down the driveway.

Buford moved his car back where it was, blocking the fence lined driveway, got out of his car, staring at the armed Indians coming towards him from two different directions.

"Thank you," said Molly softly, viewing the enemies advancing from two directions. "Alvin had urgent business to attend to up in the city – he's not needed here now."

"I wonder," said Buford, looking intently at Molly. "Why – Alvin – all of a sudden had urgent business up in the city?"

"I just told him what a bird told me," said Molly, smiling. "Oh, I see our guest have arrived."

Molly sat down on the bumper of Buford's car – "Son," said Molly softly. "It's time to call in the Calvary."

"Caw! Caw! Caw! Hello! Hello! Delbert Hello! Buford Hello!" yelled Jimbo standing near Buford.

Soon a good number of noisy crows began to congregate in the nearby trees – both of the warring parties slowed, then stopped, their advances. Looking intently at the arriving evil spirits.

"Caw! Caw! Caw! Hello! Hello! Delbert Hello! Buford Hello!" Jimbo yelled again.

Jim and Bruce were just standing there in disbelief, as a multitude of crows continued to arrive. "Jim – Bruce" said Molly softly. "Would you mind setting with me in the car for a few minutes, - we're not needed now."

Instantly Jim and Bruce were in Buford's car – "Handsome law men," said Molly quietly – "You can stand out front and address the advancing tribe – remember – at the proper moment to stand perfectly still – those heathens believe you're the ghost of Delbert Mucks – make the most of it!"

Buford made a few steps toward the advancing mob, put his thumbs in his belt, looking toward the ground, as the mob advanced at last- Buford looked up staring at the mob – "You men," ordered Buford –"Stop this foolishment! – Go home now!"

"You evil spirit" "Evil...." "Evil..." yelled several advancing Indians, as they neared Buford standing thumbs in belt unmoving.

Now you men back off! – Go home! – Now – Demanded Buford.

"You evil spirit," yelled several Indians shaking their fist – "You evil Ghost Spirit!"

"Big Buck! Sly Wolf! Take your men back home – now," demanded Buford now pointing at the two old men leading the mob – I'm Buford Nitch, Shadeys Constable – Now go home – Now I'm ordering you!"

From both directions, the superstitious Indians, gingerly began to advance toward where Buford was standing all the time keeping weary eyes on the arriving crows.

"Auk! Auk! Hello Buford! Auk! Auk!" yelled Jimbo standing near the car.

At that cry of Jimbo, a multitude of crows began to swoop in and attack both bands of Indians threatening Buford.

In an instant, both bands of potential combatants were trying to shelter from the crow attack – some were laying prostrate holding their heads or swatting at the birds – some were crawling – some were running – all were yelling trying to go back the way they came.

When the pandemonium had at last subsided, Buford with Jimbo standing behind him were still frozen to the ground – with Fred setting on Buford's shoulder nibbling on his ear, in full view of everyone within eyesight.

"Caw! Caw! Caw!" commanded Jimbo in a loud voice! Soon the attacks began to subside.

"That's enough," said Jimbo in a normal voice. "You can go home now."

Fred took flight, back toward what used to be the lab – most of the crows followed him. A few however, lit in the nearby trees appearing to be doing guard duty.

"That worked out nicely," said Molly smiling that radiant smile, after emerging from Buford's car. "No one seems to be much worse off for their troubles – maybe we've all learned our lessons. Maybe Delbert's work with the crows wasn't in vain after all."

"If I hadn't seen this, with my own eyes, I wouldn't have believed any of this," said Jim looking at Molly and Jimbo.

"Even after reading about the possibilities in Muck's books – I just couldn't believe such things were possible – that was – without a doubt – the damnedest demonstration of a controlled animal behavior I've ever seen or heard tell of! How could anyone explain what we've just seen?"

"You can't," said Molly. "That's why Delbert had to work, mostly in silence – only a very few people could believe what you've just seen." Maybe those renegades have been made believers now – those crows are not evil spirits – they're trained animals anyway – my hats off to Delbert," said Buford shaking his head.

"Mine too," said Bruce. "Maybe seeing is believing, what I've just seen. No one I know would believe me if I told them – but we've seen it!"

"Maybe now we can get back to peace and tranquility again," said Molly smiling. "Maybe me and Jimbo can rebuild the lab and continue Delberts work! You, handsome law man, with the help of crows, can keep order around here."

"Maybe I can help you," said Bruce smiling at Molly.

"Maybe you can," said Molly. "We'd appreciate any real help we could get – and you – handsome law man – maybe you better take your wife, you've been neglecting lately, on a nice anniversary vacation."

"Molly," Buford asked looking intently at her, "do I dare ask what happened here? – and my wife, do you know her?"

"Not exactly," said Molly, "but I know you and the Delberts of this world. You get so deep in the forests of your work, you can't see a lovely tree any more that's standing beside you."

"You're probably right," said Buford looking at the ground. "I got to ask you – you seemed to know a lot more about this whole situation than I do – can I ask why?"

"Jimbo and I just listen to the crows – this really concern them too – this was their home too – especially the young ones. Those crows knew in an instant when someone came around that was a threat to them, - and they told Jimbo, yesterday, just like they used to tell Delbert – and they told you - if you were listening?"

"Un huh," said Buford thoughtfully – the crows – did they tell you who did this – who set those fires?"

"They didn't have a word for their names, but they knew where they lived – and that they were a threat to crows," said Molly smiling – "They are Indians – and they live a way out east, on the reservation – they also are the ones that throwed Harley back in the river. Those Indians have killed crows for their feathers – they are the ones that helped Harley. Oh – and next time you see Bobby Davis and Little Wolf, ask them how they just happened to find Harley, in the water, there by that old bridge Butress. Seems the crows sorta showed them the way.

"Uh huh," said Buford looking intently at Molly. "I will – and – Moses – Joe – Shoo – what'd they have to do with all this?"

"I'm guessing now," said Molly smiling. "Probably nothing – the crows weren't concerned with them on their presence – I'm guessing they were telling the truth. They told James, Buella sent her nephews after her husband – before he got into trouble – they probably got there too late – Harley was probably already dead – if I had to guess."

"Uh huh," said Buford still looking at Molly. "It's astounding – absolutely astounding – yours and Mona's guess work? – Why is it so accurate?"

"Oh, that simple," said Molly smiling. "You men – around Shadey – don't listen to the wind blow – the birds' chirp – nor to reason – until it hits you upside your head. Mona – according to Bruce – listens to the wind blow. So does Bruce – in his store. Here's the difference – you men add one and one and get two – Mona adds – one and one – that makes three or four sometimes – it's woman's math – it's beyond most men."

"Oh Lord, not you too?" said Buford shaking his head smiling. Now looking at Jim, Bruce, and Jimbo standing listening to Molly – did you men learn anything?"

"I have," said Bruce smiling. "I now know I waste my time working – I should have gone to her school."

"It's getting late," said Molly. "If you don't mind, Jimbo and I will head back across the river – the long way – tomorrow we'll be over at the lab seeing what needs to be done."

"I'd like to help," said Bruce.

"Me too," said Jim.

"Thanks for the offer," said Molly. "Oh, I nearly forgot – Otto mentioned something about a Sheriff and six deputies on their way over here – I guess I am getting forgetful. We can talk about this some other time – it's getting late."

"Maybe we better go head off the posse," said Jim to Buford. "It seems the war is over for the moment."

"Molly, I don't know how to thank you," said Buford. "How can I repay you?"

"Take your wife on a romantic vacation," said Molly smiling. "We'll talk when you get back – oh Kate, Mona, Eva, and Mitch rends were some of my students when I was teaching biology and zoology in Ada years ago – So was Effee Mims and Kathy Thomas – we were young back then – at least they were."

## *Chapter 20 The End*

The old adage – the more things change, "the more they remain the same," certainly applies to the old, out of the way, small community, like Shadey.

In the small community of Shadey – still – a way off the beaten path, life began to return to normal. The week or so of intense excitement – subsided – and soon faded into ancient history. The removal of bones of Delbert Mick to Reachery and the burial of Harley Fritzs, soon were lost in the everyday hub bub of Shadies citizens.

It became apparent early on, that the predators of the crime and arson, on both sides of the river, fell into the jurisdiction of the federal agencies of Indian affairs.

The investigation by the federal government drug on for weeks. At last report, the investigation was unresolved and continuing.

The drowning of Harley Fritzs has remained unsolved – citing lack of evidence. Whether his drowning was intentional, as many of the Indians on the south side of the river maintained to appease the spirits of their dead, or was an unfortunate accident, as suggested by the young, unreliable witnesses.

The unsubstantiated claim that there was a substantial gash on the head of Harley, as of yet, is still unverified. All attempts to exhume the body for autopsy had been denied in District Court – before the District Judge Alvin Thomas.

The sworn testimonies of Constable James Dobbs of Reachery, were dismissed as irrelevant by federal authorities. The incidents of unusual crow behavior, cited as relevant by both constables were dismissed, then ridiculed as fabrications. The constables were unable to produce, concrete, tangible, and reliable proof – only hearsay – attributed to the old men – of dubious qualifications and character, because of their age and reluctance to testify.

The recognized, local biologist Jimbo Mucks and the doctor of zoology, Molly Grubs were never called to testify in the federal, arson investigation. Nor were the three books, by the renounced scientist Delbert Mucks, now deceased, cited as possible proof of a controlled, documented, animal behavior.

The federal investigation dragged on – going nowhere – bogged down in burocratic technicalities. The young man, Jimbo Mucks, announced his intention to continue his fathers' dedicated, momental work and to rebuild his father's lab.

The ageing Mayor Jim Bohannan and longtime Councilman Bruce Adams with the able assistance of James Dobbs of Reachery and Buford Nitch of Shadey volunteered their talents and resolves in the young man's endeavors to continue Delbert Mucks research in isolation.

Molly Grubs took another one of her absences, to her home back east, and has only been seen, occasionally in Reachery and Shadey to visit with her son and old friends.

Buford Nitch retired at the end of his twenty-two years of service as constable, having taken Molly's advice, he took Kate, his wife on an extended romantic vacation. The Nitches returned to their home on the out skirts of Shadey and began their retirement years.

Now retired, with time on their hands Buford and Kate volunteered to assist the young biologist, now restoring the lab. In time, it was rumored there was "a something" out west of the cemetery, down the lane west of cemetery behind that locked gate and no trespassing sign.

A number of Indians, on both sides of the river, at first, avoided Buford, now often seen visiting with old friends in both Shadey and Reachery. Many of the older Indians were convinced, the evil spirit of Delbert Mucks, now rested on the former constable of Shadey. Cited as proof, was the number of crows that congregated in the timber neat Nitche's home.

Occasionally, down at city hall, a complaint would be filed about the crows, but they became fewer, with the passing of time. Most of the complaints came from fishermen, trying to walk the riverbanks that had ventured too far west on the posted property.

Most of Shadeys residents had heard ghost talking at some time, several had experienced seeing some rather unusual behavior from crafty crows. Many of Shadeys citizens kept a warry eye upon the where abouts of the crow population. That would put a knot on back of the head of unsuspecting citizens.

<<>><<>><<>>

For a while, a train going through town, once in a while was note worthy, but in time, the railroad was abandoned, and the right of way became over grown weeds and bushes. The school was closed, and the old Indian rights advocate, Effee Mims moved to the city.

There were still a few Indians and their superstitions on the reservation east of town, but now a new interstate separate Shadey and the reservation.

The half dozen Indians that still resided around Shadey, stayed pretty well to themselves. The old widow Buella Fritzs and her brother, the town drunk, Moses Sun Song, still kept a vigilant watch that note of their buried ancestors' graves were disturbed by archeologist's, vandals, evil spirits, ghost or court orders.

From time to time, a dirty unkept man, was seen pushing a wheelbarrow, down Main Street, in full view of the few Shadey citizens that remained.

The recluse had been known to spend considerable time, occasionally if old Bruce was there, in the Johnny Adams Convince and Feed Store and Gas Station, the only business now in town since Mona's café closed.

A few weeks before Mona closed her café, the old friends Jim Bohannan, former mayor, Buford Nitch, former constable, and Bruce Adams were setting in Mona's Café, talking about old times when the recluse pushed his wheelbarrow into town. He had stopped at the convenience store and was making his way to the post office, when Mona looking out the window announced. "Jimbo's in town."

The three men rushed out the door, crowed the street, and surrounded the recluse, underneath the tree in front of the post office. Soon a number of crows began to arrive.

"Well hello there," said Buford. "It's nice to see you again."

"Hello Delbert, hello Delbert," said a crow.

The men stood there grinning when a crow lit on Bufords shoulder, eyeing his shirt pocket, after nibbling his ear.

Buford produced a few grains of corn, "Well hello Fred."

"Hello Delbert," said the crow.

"Hello Buford, Hello Buford," said Buford grinning, "nice to see you again."

"Hello Bu – Buf – Buford," said the crow, "hello Delbert."

"That's not Fred, said Jimbo grinning – "I call him Mouth, that's Fred's grandson."

The bird flew back into the tree, kit on a low limb and began to caw, "damn Buford damn – damn Buford damn- hello Delbert hello."

"That's enough," said Jimbo softly. "Can you show Buford please?"

The bird lit at Buford's feet, flopped upside sown and began to plead, "please – please – please."

"Can you do better than that?" asked Buford, "beg."

The bird righted itself, lowered its head and began to beg – "please – please – please."

Buford produced some grains of corn – "Can you dance?' The bird began to sway from side to side, shaking its tail.

"Please, please," said the bird.

Buford presented the bird his well-earned treats – "Well I'll be damned."

Bruce and Jim stood like statues watching the show.

"No one I know would believe this," said Bruce grinning.

"I would," yelled Mona, standing out front of her café grinning from ear to ear. – "I expect to read a detailed account of what I've just seen, in the book, Kate tells me you're writing!"

Made in the USA
Middletown, DE
03 September 2024

60267150R00126